Blue Sky
STUDIOS

Rio 2

HarperFestival is an imprint of HarperCollins Publishers.

Rio 2: The Junior Novel

Printed in the United States of America.

www.harpercollinschildrens.com

Library of Congress catalog card number: 2013956394
ISBN 978-0-06-228504-1

Book design by Victor Joseph Ochoa
14 15 16 17 OPM 10 9 8 7 6 5 4 3 2
❖
First Edition

THE JUNIOR NOVEL

Adapted by Christa Roberts

HARPER FESTIVAL
An Imprint of HarperCollinsPublishers

Chapter 1

In the magical city of Rio de Janeiro, a party was taking place. Children were waving sparklers. Couples were dancing to vibrant Brazilian rhythms. Cruise ships filled with guests in the party spirit were docked in the bay off Copacabana Beach. Everyone was getting into the groove, laughing and making wishes as they tossed flowers into the ocean. Because tonight's celebration wasn't just any party—it was New Year's Eve. And no one was happier than a rare blue Spix's Macaw named Blu.

High up on Corcovado Mountain in the shadows of the Cristo Redentor statue, birds of all colors swirled and partied together. Nico, a yellow canary, and Pedro, a red-crested cardinal, were spinning the tunes. Catchy tunes with hot, upbeat tempos. Blu knew he wasn't the best dancer. But he definitely had the best dance partner he could ever ask for–his wife, Jewel.

"For a bird from Minnesota you've got some moves," Jewel said as Blu dipped her on the crowded dance floor.

"Oh, actually that wasn't a move." Blu smiled back at his wife. "That was an accident. But I accept the compliment."

The couple twirled in time to the music.

Blu had been the last male of his species until his caretaker, Linda, brought him from their home in Minnesota to an aviary in Rio owned by Tulio Monteiro, a Brazilian ornithologist. There, Blu met and fell in love with Jewel, a female blue Spix's Macaw. Now they had three children together, and lived in a sanctuary Linda and Tulio created.

Life was pretty good.

"It's great Rafael could watch the kids," Jewel said as they bopped to the beat.

Blu nodded, shaking his bright blue tail feathers. "Yeah, looks like you're stuck with me all night."

Jewel smiled back adoringly. "And I couldn't be happier. You're my one and only, Blu."

Blu narrowly missed stepping on Jewel's toe. "Ah, that's a good thing. Since I'm the only other one." It was a running joke between them. No other blue Spix's Macaws existed in the world.

"Hey, ya lovebirds!" Blu and Jewel turned at the sound of a familiar voice. It was their friend Rafael, a Toco toucan, with his wife, Eva, a keel-billed toucan.

Rafael's yellow-orange bill gleamed in the moonlight. "Happy New Year!"

But if Rafael and Eva were here, Blu thought, where were his kids?

"Raffi?" Blu began worriedly. "Where are–"

Rafael held out one of his black wings. "The kids are with Luiz. No worries."

"Worries, right here!" Blu said nervously, tapping himself on his chest. Immediately Blu and Jewel looked across the dancing crowd, searching, searching. . . . Then, Blu spotted Luiz the bulldog, boogying to the beat. Dog drool was flying everywhere. But the kids were nowhere to be seen.

Trying not to panic, Blu and Jewel hurried over to Luiz.

"Luiz!" Blu said, dodging a spittle of drool. "Where are the kids?"

Luiz gazed up at them. "What? I don't have any kids."

"Our kids!" Blu and Jewel shouted.

"Oh, right," Luiz said, getting it. "I left them with Tiny."

"Tiny!" they repeated, horrified.

Luiz was taken aback. "What? She's an excellent babysitter."

Blu and Jewel knew their kids would love staying with Tiny. They hoped she felt the same way!

"I'm a terrible babysitter," said Tiny, a small green bird. She had agreed to let the kids tie her to a large bottle rocket–and to them putting on a fireworks display—but now, she wasn't sure it was the best idea.

"This is gonna be awesome!" Tiago assured her. He was the youngest, and the only boy. Right now he was zipping around jamming fireworks into the ground. His bookish sister Bia was working out the details for their own New Year's spectacle here at the base of Corcovado.

"All right, I've done all the calculations and each explosion will be perfectly synced to the beat," she said confidently. "Unless . . . I didn't carry the one."

Over to the side, Carla, the oldest and most artistic of the three kids, was sharing her opinion. "Here's my vision: red, blue, green, yellow, yellow, purple!"

"Here's my vision," Tiago declared. He held a lit match. "Boom! Pow! Bang! KAPOW!" He tore across Bia's drawings.

Worry lines creased Tiny's forehead. "I don't think your parents would like this very much," she warned Tiago.

And no sooner were the words out of her mouth

than Blu and Jewel flew in and landed.

"Whoa, whoa, whoa," Jewel said as Tiago ran by with the match. She grabbed him by his tail feathers while Blu took the lit match. "Where you going, little bird?"

"What is this?" Blu let out an exasperated sigh. "Guys, you know the rules. No pyrotechnics without adult supervision."

Bia shrugged. "We asked Tiny."

"That's even worse," Blu scolded. "Sorry, Tiny."

Tiny hung her head in shame. She was still tied to the rocket. "You don't have to pay me, Señor Blu."

Blu took the rest of the fireworks out of Carla's hand. "Kids, next time, ask me."

"But you always say no," Carla complained.

Blu looked at his daughter. "No, I don't."

"Dad, you're in denial!" Tiago blurted out.

Blu turned to his wife for backup. "Okay, honey, do I always say no?"

Jewel shook her head. "Yes. I mean . . . uh . . . no."

Carla snorted. "Great. Now Mom's saying it too."

"Do you know how dangerous this is?" he asked. The match flame singed Blu's talons and he dropped it. Tiago nodded enthusiastically, making Blu groan. How many times did he have to tell them? "Listen, we're the last blue Spix's Macaws left on the planet," he reminded his family. "We have to stay safe! Birds of blue feathers . . ."

"Have to stick together!" the kids finished with him.

Carla's beak twitched. "I smell chicken," she said, sniffing.

"I could eat," Tiago said.

It wasn't chicken . . . it was Blu's tail feathers! The dropped match had lit them on fire!

"No, no, no, no, no!" Blu cried, darting back and forth as he tried to put out the flames.

Bia folded her wings. "By my calculations that's like his twenty-seventh 'no' today!"

As Blu shook out his flaming feathers, a few of

them fell off and fluttered to the ground, landing on top of the fireworks Bia and Tiago had set up.

Ssssst. The fireworks ignited. Including the one Tiny was strapped to. The small green bird frantically tried to blow out the lit fuse.

Oh, no! Blu ran over to help her. Luckily he was able to free Tiny from the rocket . . . but unluckily, he got caught on the roman candle himself. He braced himself for what was coming next. *Five, four, three, two . . .* "Everybody fly!" he shouted. "Happy new year!"

His family moved out of the way as Blu was launched into the sky. A few seconds later, Blu dropped back to earth, landing on the arm of the Cristo Redentor statue beside his family. "Well, this year's off to a great start," he said as fireworks filled the night sky to the delight of the kids.

Little did Blu and Jewel know, as their children gathered around them, that their greatest adventure was about to begin.

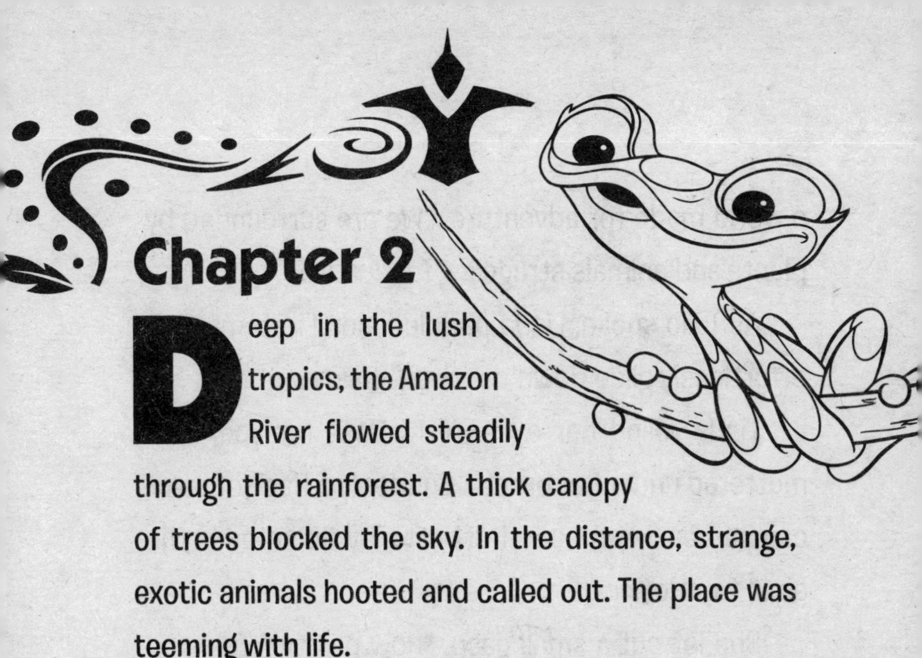

Chapter 2

Deep in the lush tropics, the Amazon River flowed steadily through the rainforest. A thick canopy of trees blocked the sky. In the distance, strange, exotic animals hooted and called out. The place was teeming with life.

A canoe glided along the river. Inside were two people–Brazilian ornithologist Tulio Monteiro and his American-born wife, Linda–and one small bird in a large birdcage.

Tulio sat in the back of the boat, holding a camcorder, recording everything. He spoke into it excitedly, thrilled by the sights and sounds of the jungle. "Amazon expedition, day seven. Two thousand miles from Rio, we've reached the center of the rain forest."

Exotic jungle sounds echoed around them. It was

a world made for adventure. "We are surrounded by plants and animals struggling for survival."

As Tulio spoke, Linda paddled along in front. "We effortlessly glide down the river," Tulio went on.

Linda rolled her eyes. "Effortless for you," she muttered under her breath. Suddenly a flash of color caught her eye. A beautiful butterfly fluttered in the air in front of her.

She let out a small gasp. "How pretty!" Then . . . *snap*! A piranha leapt out of the water and chomped on the butterfly.

"Oooh, spit it out!" Linda yelped, scuttling back in her seat. "Spit it out!"

But the piranha, ignoring her, had already dropped back into the water.

Tulio gave her a blissful smile. "Ah, the savage beauty of the circle of life."

Linda paddled on as Tulio continued.

"We are near the nesting grounds of the Amazonian wood quail. *Odontophorus gujanensis*. Six months ago, we rescued this little bird from smugglers. It was sick, malnourished, with a broken leg. But now, my trusty assistant–"

Linda shot him a look.

"I mean, loving wife and colleague," Tulio corrected himself, grinning guiltily at Linda, "will now release her back to her natural habitat."

They had reached the riverbank. Linda opened the birdcage. The little bird stood there, shaking a little.

"It's okay," Linda told it. "You can go now. Just like this." She flapped her arms up and down.

"Let me talk to her," Tulio said. "Hoooo-hoo!" he said, mimicking a bird. "Hoooo-hoo!"

"Go on," Linda encouraged.

Slowly, the little bird stepped out of the cage and gave a few squawks.

"Do you think she's gonna be all right?" Linda asked, concerned. The little bird didn't look too sure of herself.

Tulio nodded. "Give her some time."

Just then, several other Amazonian wood quails emerged from the jungle. Linda and Tulio watched from the canoe, touched, as the other quails made a circle around the little one and welcomed her.

"Welcome home," Linda whispered as the little bird headed into the brush with her new friends. But then, to Tulio's surprise, just as quickly as she'd gone into the jungle she came out again, squawking urgently.

"Wait a minute. What is she saying, Tulio?" Linda asked as the little bird made frantic motions with her wings. The boat began to drift down the river.

"They imprint on me so strongly, you know," he said, smiling at the little bird. "It's just hard for her to say good-bye."

Linda wasn't so sure. "No, I think it's . . . I think she's trying to warn us," she said as the bird's motions grew more and more frantic.

"No, no, no, Linda," Tulio insisted. "It might be

some sort of mating dance."

By now the little bird was running in circles, pointing and squawking. Suddenly Linda realized that the canoe was drifting faster down the river. She grabbed the sides of the canoe as it sailed wildly through the water. "Tulio! Look!"

In the quickly approaching distance, Tulio could hear what sounded like a dull roar.

"Paddle!" Linda yelled, grabbing her paddle and digging it into the churning water.

"Now!" The peaceful Amazon River they'd cruised down this morning was leading them to rapids!

Tulio fumbled for a paddle and quickly began paddling against the surge. "Oh! Okay, okay! Paddle! Watch out!" he cried as the paddle slipped from his grasp into the rushing water. He began shouting directions to Linda. "Paddle! Paddle! Backward! Backward! To the right! No, no, left!" He gulped air. "Forward! Forward!" he shouted. "No, no, no! Backward!"

Linda was doing her best, but it was impossible.

"Make up your mind, Tulio!" she shrieked.

It was too late. They charged down the rapids. Linda tried to push away from the rocks, jamming the oar in between them, but–*snap!*–the oar broke in half.

"Cheese and sprinkles!" Linda shrieked, her eyes widening in horror. The boat careened out of control. Spinning, the canoe went backward over the falls.

"Tulio!" Linda cried as she and Tulio were catapulted out of the canoe and swept under the rushing water.

✿ ✿ ✿ ✿ ✿

Downriver, the capsized canoe gently floated by. Tulio had surfaced, gasping for air. In his hands he still held his camera. Grabbing onto a rock, he pulled himself onto the bank. "Linda! Linda!"

"Tulio!" Linda shouted. She emerged from the bushes, wrapped up in vines and covered with sticks and leaves. "Ugh. Yuck." She tried to wipe the gunk off her body. "Thank heavens you're okay." They hugged each other, relieved.

A loud squawk rang out in the rain forest, catching their attention.

"Tulio, is that a–"

He motioned for her to stay quiet. Then, he crept forward toward the bushes and raised his camera to try and snap a picture.

A blue streak flashed past them, startling Tulio enough that he dropped his camera in the river. A bright blue feather floated down and settled nearby. His eyes wide, Tulio picked up the feather, blew on it, and stuck his tongue out to taste the end.

"Linda, this is incredible!" he said excitedly, handing her the feather. This wasn't just any feather. It belonged to a blue macaw!

Meanwhile, back in Rio, Jewel glided through the air over Guanabara Bay, filled with joy. In her beak she clutched a large Brazil nut . . . a perfect breakfast.

Soaring over the lagoon, she gazed out on the city below her. Street vendors were moving in and out of stopped traffic in the morning rush hour. Tourists with their maps and cameras were filling the streets and going in and out of buildings. Humans were busy doing the things that humans did.

Jewel was glad she was a macaw.

Flying to the bird conservatory, she glided over the observation tower and swooped past Fernando. He was sixteen now, and looked after birds from the surrounding jungle.

"Good morning, Jewel!" he called out, waving as she squawked hello. Soon she came to a manmade birdhouse that sat atop a tall pole next to Linda and Tulio's cottage. There was one main room, and three smaller rooms that had been added on over the years.

It was home.

Jewel landed outside the main box and poked her head inside. "Hey everyone, look what I found!"

No one answered her. "Blu?" she called. "Kids?" She peeked in the other boxes. They were empty.

"Where did everybody go?"

The sound of clanging pots and a blaring television caught her attention. It was coming from Linda and Tulio's cottage. A window was open.

"Who's ready for some breakfast?" she heard Blu say.

She shook her head. "Unbelievable."

The kitchen was all hustle and bustle. Blu manned the griddle, flipping pancakes like a professional chef.

"Did you know that these whole wheat pancakes have twice the vitamins and minerals of regular pancakes?" Bia said, studying the box of pancake mix Blu had placed on the counter.

"And with the blueberries it's four times as tasty," Blu added, whistling. He popped open the fridge. "Hey, where are the blueberries?"

"Oh, Dad!" Tiago tossed a blueberry in the air. "Looking for this?"

Blu's eyes narrowed. He knew what Tiago was

doing. He was throwing down a challenge.

"Bring it," Blu said.

Tiago passed the blueberry to his father.

Blu pulled off some fancy footwork. "It's down to the final minutes. He's got magic in his feet. He shoots!" He popped the berry into the air and did a bicycle kick, catapulting it into the pancake batter. "He scores!"

"*Goallllllll!*" he and Bia shouted together. Blu did a celebratory dance.

Getting into the spirit, Tiago lined the rest of the blueberries up, took aim, and began kicking them to Blu. "Heads up, Dad!"

Blu could handle one berry. But this was too much. Blueberries flew at him left and right. He tried to kick them all into the pancakes, but instead, he tripped and fell, sending a pancake flying across the room. *Splat!* It hit the wall next to the window. The window where Jewel sat, looking less than amused. She blinked three times.

"Uh-oh. The three blink," Bia said. "Mom's mad. Time to go."

"Hey, honey!" Blu said, catching his breath. "Are you hungry?"

Jewel flew into the room, still holding the Brazil nut. "Blu, we talked about this."

The kids watched their parents. "Neck twist," Carla said as Blu fidgeted. "Change of subject."

"Ummm, so, uhhh, so whatta you got there?" Blu managed to say.

"Breakfast," she told him, irritated.

"That's funny," Blu said, grinning. "But, seriously, what is that?"

Jewel dropped it on the counter. "It's a Brazil nut. I never thought I'd find one this close to the city. I want to show the kids how to open one."

"You mean like this?" Tiago blurted out. He popped open a can of Brazil nuts, causing his mother to groan. "Dad already showed us."

Jewel looked at Blu, but before she could say

anything, Carla let out a squeal.

"Wait! Wait . . . wait, go back! Mom! Dad!" she interrupted. "You're on TV!"

The family gathered around the television set. A reporter was interviewing Tulio.

"Doctor Tulio Monteiro, the 'Bird Man of Brazil,' announced an important discovery today," the reporter said. The camera flashed to Tulio.

Tulio nodded, holding up a blue feather. "We believe we have encountered a wild blue Spix's Macaw deep in the Amazon jungle."

"The blue Spix's Macaw was thought to be practically extinct," the reporter chimed in, "with the last remaining family living under protection at the Blu Bird Sanctuary in Rio de Janiero." Pictures of Blu, Jewel, and the kids flashed onto the screen.

"We're famous!" Carla said excitedly.

The scene flashed back to Tulio and Linda at their camp in the Amazon. "There may be a whole flock out there," Tulio said. "And if there is, we will find them and protect them!"

Tulio pulled Linda close as she waved at the camera. "Hi, Blu."

"Hi, Linda!" Blu said to the TV. They were still waving as the camera pulled away.

Jewel gazed at her family in amazement. "We're not the only ones! There are more of us out there!"

"Yeah, that's great. I'm sure there–"

"All this time, I thought we were all alone," Jewel said to herself.

"Hey, it hasn't been all bad," Blu protested.

Jewel turned to him. "Of course not! But just imagine if there was a whole flock of us." Jewel flew over to the window and looked outside, lost in thought. "How amazing would that be?" Her mind was racing. "We've got to do something!"

Blu gaped at her. "We do?"

Jewel's excitement was growing. "Yeah! We have to fly to the Amazon and help Linda and Tulio find them!" She hopped from foot to foot.

"Whoa. Whoa, whoa," Blu put his wings up. Now she was getting ahead of herself. "We can't just pack up and go."

"Why not?" Jewel asked. "It's about time this family got a little air under our wings." She zoomed in the air toward the startled kids, snatching away their gadgets. "Look at us! iPods. TV! Pancakes! We're not people. We're *birds*."

"Hey!" Carla cried as her iPod was ripped from her talons.

"Mom!" Bia and Tiago exclaimed as their mother flew around the room, a bird on a mission.

"We have to get out to the wild and be birds, Blu!" she told her husband, zooming over to him. "Let the kids connect to their roots. Show them what I had."

There was a spark in Jewel's eyes that Blu had never seen before. "They need this," Jewel went on, passionate. "*We* need this. Come on, Blu. What do you say?"

He hesitated. "I don't know. Maybe . . . uhhh . . ."

"He didn't say no!" Carla exclaimed.

"Which means he practically said yes!" Bia added excitedly.

Things were moving too fast. "Hey. Wait a second—"

"It's gonna be so much fun!" Jewel exclaimed.

Tiago did a wing pump. "Yeahhhhhh! We're going to the *Amazon*!" Then he looked at his parents. "What's the Amazon?"

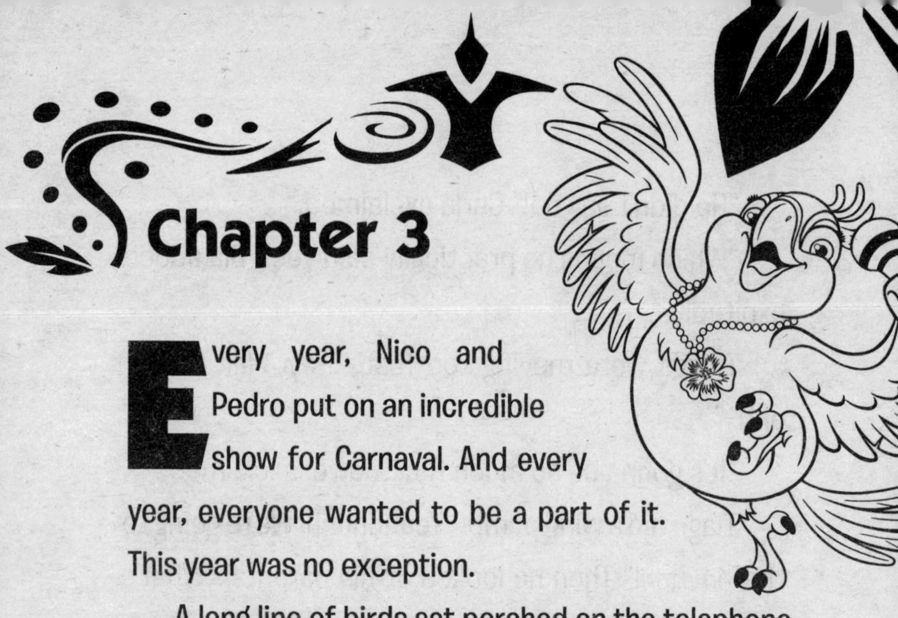

Chapter 3

Every year, Nico and Pedro put on an incredible show for Carnaval. And every year, everyone wanted to be a part of it. This year was no exception.

A long line of birds sat perched on the telephone wires outside Luiz's garage. Pigeons and parakeets, doves and hummingbirds and cuckoos all mingled together, doing vocal exercises and getting ready for their moment to shine.

"Next!" Luiz called. He was working the entrance door. A tall, long-legged spoonbill confidently looked at the other contenders.

"That would be me," he said cockily. "Okay, everyone can go home now. You're looking at the next King of Carnaval!"

He flew through the door and landed next to Luiz.

"Hey, big bird, break a leg!" Luiz said encouragingly. As the bird walked inside, he slipped on Luiz's drool and fell down.

Luiz winced. "Ooooh! Walk it off, buddy!"

It was audition time, and Eva had just finished belting out a rousing song. From the judge's table, Nico and Pedro stared at her openmouthed. Rafael was hanging on every note. Rafael smiled and clapped energetically. Then he flew over to her side.

"Bravo! Bravo! Bravo! That was amazing! Eva, darling, you hit every note!" He turned to look at Nico and Pedro. "Huh, guys?"

"Yeah, yeah, with a bunch of notes I never heard of," Pedro muttered under his breath.

Eva was looking eagerly at the judges. "So, am I going to be in your Carnaval production this year? Hmmm?"

Nico and Pedro looked at each other. Neither of them knew what to say.

Pedro spoke first. "Yeah, yeah, we'll get back to you," he told her.

"Uh, Rafael has your contact info, right?" Nico asked.

Eva sensed that they weren't being truthful with her. "Raffi!" She turned to her husband for help. He ushered her out.

"Don't worry," he assured her as she glared at him. "I'll talk to them. We'll find the perfect spot for you."

"In Ecuador, maybe," Nico mumbled.

"You better," Eva said to Rafael threateningly. Then she turned back to Nico and Pedro. "Ciao, ciao. Bye, boys!" And with a wave, the opera-singing toucan flew off.

"See you back at home, my tasty mango!" Rafael called after her.

Nico sighed. "None of the acts are inspiring. I'm just not inspired. Carnaval is right around the corner and our reputations are on the line."

"Copy that," Pedro agreed. "We need something

that can make us wiggle. Something to make us jiggle. We need something that pops! Pop, pop, pop, pop, pop! You know what pop is backwards? Pop!"

Nico knew his friend was right. "Next!" he barked, hoping greatness would walk through the door.

It was the spoonbill. He wiped the drool off himself. "Ew, disgusting. Gentlemen, I'm your–"

"Whoa!" Blu slipped in a puddle of Luiz's drool and slid into the spoonbill. *Crash!* Blu and the spoonbill untangled themselves. The spoonbill flew up and landed on the hood of a car, away from the commotion. He looked irritated.

"Sorry bro!" Luiz said, indicating the puddle of drool the macaw had slipped in.

"It's okay, Luiz," Blu said. "Good to see you too."

Pedro faced his friend. "Listen, Blu, we're looking for a singer, a dancer . . . the whole package."

"Yeah, and you're more of a mumbler-shuffler," Nico told him. "You catch my drift?"

"Oh, no, no," Blu said quickly. "I'm not here to

audition. I've got news. I am going to the Amazon. Yay . . ."

Nico looked confused. "Ama-what?"

Rafael motioned for a break. "Oooh, okay. Uhh, let's take five."

The spoonbill was frustrated. "What?" he shouted, stomping his foot. The hood of the car he was on popped open and slammed him in the face.

Blu and his buddies gathered on the garage rooftop, and he laid out his plan: he and Jewel were taking the kids to the Amazon so they could learn to live like real birds.

"The Amazon." Luiz whistled, shaking his head in amazement. "Wow. That's wild."

Blu took a deep breath. "Yeah, yeah. Jewel thinks it'll be good for us." Then he paused. "Uhhh, how . . . how wild?"

"Real wild," Luiz said.

"They got mosquitoes that suck your blood like

Slurpees," Pedro said, dropping his voice.

Nico nodded. "Snakes that can swallow you whole."

Luiz stared off into space. "Flesh-eating piranhas that eat . . . flesh," he whispered.

None of this was making Blu feel good about the decision. "Oh, great. That sounds really nice," he said sarcastically. He let out a shiver. "I'm not going."

Rafael stepped forward, holding out his wings. "Guys, guys, guys," he said, shushing them. "Blu, you have nothing to worry about. All those stories are highly exaggerated."

Blu gave him a dubious look. "You think so?"

"Of course," Rafael assured him. "If this is important to Jewel, just do it." He winked. "Happy wife, happy life. Remember that."

Happy wife, happy life, Blu repeated to himself, trying to rally his spirits. "Okay, yeah, you're right," he said. "You know, a little family vacation . . . might actually be fun," he went on, trying to convince himself.

"Plus, it's not like it's forever."

Rafael clapped him hard on the back. "That's the spirit!"

"Yeah. Okay, thanks guys," Blu said, nodding as he spoke. He'd managed to talk himself into it. He tried to put on a brave smile as he flew off. "See you in a couple of weeks!"

"Safe travels, Blu!" Rafael called after him.

"Bring me back a souvenir!" Luiz urged as Blu disappeared from view.

Rafael sighed. "He's dead."

Nico shrugged. "Too bad. Nice guy."

Rafael gazed into the horizon where Blu had flown off. Pedro and Nico's words worried him because he knew there was some truth to them.

Blu didn't know the first thing about living in the wild. But Rafael thought there was a way he could help. . . .

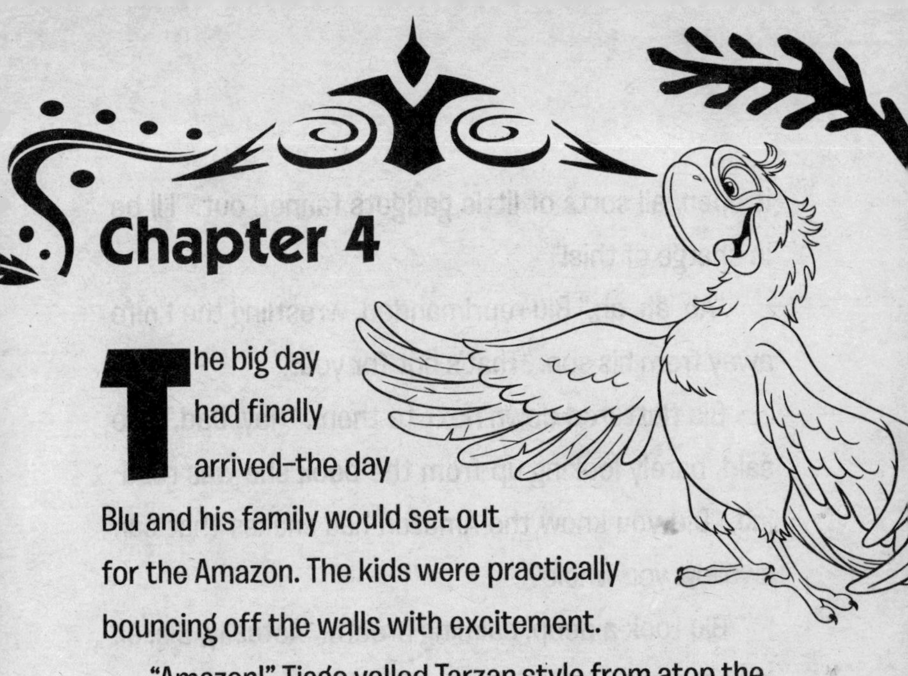

Chapter 4

The big day had finally arrived—the day Blu and his family would set out for the Amazon. The kids were practically bouncing off the walls with excitement.

"Amazon!" Tiago yelled Tarzan style from atop the birdhouse. He snapped on a pair of flying goggles and zoomed down to the opening. "Let's go! C'mon, Dad! C'mon!"

Blu stepped out, trying not to let his nerves get the best of him. "Okay. Bug spray, check. Water purifier, check. Band-Aids . . . I feel like I'm forgetting something."

Tiago rummaged around in the fanny pack Blu wore and pulled out a small tool. "Oh, cool!" he cried. "The all-in-one Adventurer's Knife!" When he popped it open, all sorts of little gadgets fanned out. "I'll be in charge of this!"

"Ah, ah, ah," Blu reprimanded, wrestling the knife away from his son. "That's not for you."

Bia fluttered down next to them. "Hey, Dad," she said, barely looking up from the book she was reading, "Did you know the Amazon has snakes that can swallow you whole?"

Blu took a deep, calming breath. "Actually, Bia, all those stories are highly exaggerated."

Bia shook her head. "No, really. Look." She spun the book around, showing Blu a photo of an enormous anaconda. The snake was bulging with what apparently was his last meal.

"Ah!" Blu gasped, horrified.

"Oh, that's sick!" Tiago said, doing a little happy dance.

Jewel joined them. "All right. We ready to go?" she asked, before her eyes lit on Blu's waist. "A fanny pack?" she said, raising an eye.

"Yeah, I need it for the GPS," Blu said firmly. "Oooh, wait, the GPS!" He dashed back into the birdhouse to find it.

Jewel was getting impatient. She wanted to get an early start and time was slipping away. "Carla!" she called. "We're leaving!"

"I'm not going," came Carla's voice from inside the birdhouse. "It's gonna be lame."

Just then Blu came back outside with the GPS. "Here it is. I programmed in Linda and Tulio's coordinates. We're all set." To prove it, he pressed a button on the device.

"Destination, Amazon," a woman's voice said. Except she had a British accent so it sounded more like "Ah-moe-zone."

Jewel cocked her head. "You trust this woman?" she asked Blu.

"Yes. I. Do." He mimicked the GPS voice with a wink, making Jewel laugh.

An approaching figure flying through the air

caught their attention. It was Rafael. "Hey, hey, wait up, family," he said, swooping down beside them. "I'm coming too."

"Don't worry, buddy," he said when he saw Blu's surprised expression. "We got your back."

"Eva let you come?" Blu asked, incredulous. Eva never let Rafael do anything.

"Sure," Rafael said easily. "I promised her a spot in the Carnaval show."

A little shriek came from above them. "You did what?" Nico cried. He and Pedro landed beside the group.

"You guys are late!" Rafael scolded the canary and the cardinal.

"*Clock* late," Nico admitted.

Pedro did a little dance. "But musician early."

Hearing the commotion, Carla stuck her head out of her room. "Wait, you guys are coming?"

Pedro held up his wings in a movie-director moment. "We wouldn't miss it for the world. We're gonna scout the wildest, coolest talent in that jungle."

Nico clutched his bottle-cap hat to his chest. "It's our inspiration for this year's Carnaval show. 'Amazon, Untamed!'"

"Cool!" Carla exclaimed. Then she caught herself. "I mean, yeah, okay, I guess I'll go."

"Amazon jungle or bust, baby!" Nico yelled, doing a little fist pump.

Pedro was busy high-fiving the kids, who were even more excited now. "Who's ready for a tropical adventure?"

"All right!" Carla said.

"Let's go, birds!" Rafael said, preparing for flight. Bia handed her book to Blu to carry in flight.

Things were moving too fast for Blu's liking. "Wait, wait!" he cried, feeling anxious. "We didn't do a head count."

But no one was waiting. Instead, Jewel was soaring into the sky, the rest of the birds taking position behind her.

"Hey, guys, wait up!" Blu yelled as he jumped into the air, his GPS device changing rapidly.

The world was an incredible place. And Blu and his family had a bird's-eye view. They flew over the city of Ouro Preto, in the Serra do Espinhaço, and perched on the bell tower of the cathedral there.

What an amazing place, Blu thought as he checked the GPS to make sure they were on track. Of course Carla was too busy listening to her iPod to notice her surroundings–and Tiago was too busy scaring them all half to death by ringing the giant bell.

But it was still a great family moment.

And who else could say that they got to ride a rhea bird? Or fly over the capital city and rest on top of the crescent-shaped Congress Dome? Or leave the city for the country, soaring over fields of wildflowers?

As night fell, they flew on, Blu with all three kids

on his back and Nico and Pedro struggling to carry a fast-asleep Rafael.

And when daybreak came, Blu spotted a wonderful sight: the tiled dome of the Manaus Opera House and the busy Amazon River harbor in the distance.

Soon their Amazon family vacation would really begin.

On a darkened stage a sulphur-crested cockatoo dressed in Elizabethan-style clothing stepped into a shaft of light. In his talons he held a small bird skull.

"To be or not to be," the cockatoo said dramatically, clutching the skull. "That is the question. Whether 'tis nobler in the mind to suffer the slings and arrows of outrageous fortune . . ."

As the cockatoo continued his monologue, Gabi, a tiny pink dart frog, watched from a glass jar in the wings.

"Ah, that's beautiful, Nigel," she said, her eyes blinking rapidly. "What does it mean?"

Nigel turned his focus to her. "Death, Gabi," he intoned. "It's about death."

Gabi swooned inside her jar. "Oh, Nigel. I love it when you get all dark and brooding."

Bang! Bang! Something had hit the roof. "Time to go to work, bird," came a not-so-pleasant-sounding voice.

Nigel threw back his small shoulders. "My audience awaits." He stepped forward onto his stage through the now open birdcage door. The shady vendor who held him captive plopped a tiny turban onto Nigel's head.

"Get your fortune told by the bird of mystery!" the man yelled out to the crowded Manaus marketplace. He was a vendor, and what he was selling was Nigel.

The birdcage sat atop the vendor's table. The marketplace was filled with incredible wares—everything from exotic fruits to native art and miracle cures for everything from back pain to weight loss.

"Poison frogs! Fire ants!" came the shouts from other vendors as they tried to attract customers. Nearby, Nigel spotted Charlie, a mute giant anteater wearing a bowler hat. He was chained to a table and tap dancing for a few unimpressed onlookers.

"Come here, learn your destiny!" the man was barking.

An annoying little boy came running over, dragging his mother behind him. "Mommy, mommy, I want one! I want a fortune!" the kid whined.

His mother, exhausted, dropped a few coins into the vendor's bucket. The vendor obliged by pulling out a small drawer filled with paper fortunes. "Welcome, madam. This amazing cockatoo will reveal your future." He poked Nigel with a stick. "All right, bird. Pick a fortune!" He prodded Nigel again. "Come on, bird!"

"You're doing great, Nigel!" Gabi said.

"Pick it already!" hissed the vendor as Nigel, humiliated, hopped forward and chose a fortune for the boy.

As he did, he noticed five small blue macaws flying over the marketplace. And then he heard a voice that made his tail feathers quiver.

"C'mon, gang! Almost there. No more flying today."

"Finally!" said a younger voice.

"We've got a boat to catch!"

The familiar voices drifted down to Nigel's disbelieving ears. His eyes widened. It couldn't be. But as he stared up at the macaws flying free, he knew it was. Everything around him disappeared as he thought back to his last encounter with that bird. Blu. The bird that had caused him so much anguish. If it wasn't for Blu, Nigel never would have been hit by that propeller. He would still have all his beautiful feathers.

He would still be able to fly.

"Come on, bird!" the vendor yelled.

The boy was pulling on the fortune in Nigel's beak. "I want my fortune!"

"You're doing great!" Gabi piped up again.

The boy's mother was getting annoyed. "What's taking so long?"

"What's the matter with you?" the vendor shrieked at Nigel.

But Nigel was lost in thought. "The bluebirds of my misery," he whispered.

The boy began to cry and Nigel slammed the child's ice-cream cone into his face.

"Hey!" The vendor, maddened, brought his stick down to whack Nigel.

And without warning, Nigel's eyes narrowed. His inner rage was boiling over.

He snapped.

Grabbing the stick from the vendor, he turned tables on the man, whacking him with the stick instead. "Nice birdie," the vendor tried soothingly, but it was no use. Nigel was like a madman, swatting the vendor over and over with the stick. He swung the man into a table, flipping it over. Bottles filled with colorful liquids and jars of powders and herbs shattered, sending up colorful puffs of dust.

Gabi's jar flew into the air. "Thank you!" she cried as it fell, shattering into a million glass shards on the ground. "I'm free!"

Gabi hopped out. She was free! "Ribbit! Ribbit!" she croaked with joy. But Gabi's freedom set the crowd into a panic. She wasn't just any frog–she was a lethal dart frog. Her poison could kill small animals . . . and humans.

The marketplace was in a panic. Tourists were running in all directions.

From his table Charlie stretched his tongue and was able to reach a broken jar of fire ants. He slurped them up and instantly his face turned red with pain. But with the pain came a huge burst of energy. *Snap!* He broke his chain.

Nigel hopped onto Charlie's back like a knight readying himself for battle. "The croaking cockatoo doth bellow for revenge!" he said dramatically. "That's Shakespeare, by the way," he told Gabi, who gazed at him in adoration.

"Without your performance, it's nothing," she said.

Nigel thought about this as Gabi hopped onto Charlie's hat. "Fair point. Onward, my trusty steed!" he commanded. And as they galloped off, a fortune fluttered to the ground amidst the broken bottles and trampled fruit.

A good time to finish up old tasks.

Chapter 5

"It's been so long," Jewel said, taking a deep, relaxed breath. She, Blu, and the rest of the gang were lounging on the rooftop of an old wooden riverboat. They cruised lazily through the beautiful, murky waters of the Amazon as the sun began to set. "I was afraid I wouldn't remember any of this. But the smell of the orchids and the earth, the sound of the water . . . it's all coming back to me."

The sounds of the jungle surrounded them and a light breeze ruffled Jewel's feathers. It felt so amazing to be here. "This air!" she went on. "It's so fresh and full." She looked back toward the receding dock the boat had departed from. "Good-bye, stinky city air!"

"Yeah, bye," Blu said, watching the dock get

smaller and smaller.

Jewel gave him a pat. "Hey, thank you for doing this. I really appreciate it."

Blu gazed at her. "I would do anything for you. You know that, right?"

"Of course I do." With a happy sigh, Jewel laid her head on Blu's shoulder and closed her eyes.

Blu smiled to himself. It was a perfect romantic moment.

"Ooohhh eeeee eeee!" Blu and Jewel turned to see Tiago, making monkey sounds. And pretty soon, the monkeys in the jungle began calling back. And then Nico and Pedro got inspired.

Nico started tapping out a rhythm and Pedro began beat-boxing and singing. Soon the whole family joined in making sounds that the jungle called back to. On the deck below, human passengers were relaxing in hammocks. Shipping crates were stacked in piles. And one of these crates contained two stowaways: Nigel and Gabi.

They waited until nightfall to break out. Nigel was first, stealthily creeping his way out of the crate like a ninja. Behind him Gabi hopped along excitedly. She jumped into a fruit basket.

"I love being on Team Nigel," she whispered. The fruit basket Gabi was in began to stir, and Gabi realized that Charlie was *in* the basket. A few pieces of fruit tumbled onto the ground. A passenger stirred in his hammock.

Nigel hummed a soft, soothing tune to lull the man back to sleep, and then turned on Gabi. "Shhhh!"

Gabi turned to Charlie. "Shhhh!" As Charlie sank back down into the fruit, Gabi and Nigel made their way up to the roof.

Bouncing and flipping over snoring humans, Gabi scaled her way to the roof through an air duct. Nigel slowly stalked up the stairs.

It didn't take long for Nigel to spot his prey. There was Blu, the source of his misery, lying fast asleep next to his wife and their three pesky kids.

"I can't think of anything more romantic than poisoning passengers on a moonlight cruise," Gabi said quietly. She was dangling from the rim of the air duct. She scraped a tiny blob of poison off her skin.

"Stop!" Nigel hissed. "That one is mine." He leaned over Blu. "Twinkle, twinkle little Blu. How I wondered, where were you? Up above the world so high . . . are you ready . . . to die?"

Blu stirred in his sleep. "Ugh, you need a Tic Tac," he mumbled.

Nigel's feathers tingled with anger. "Even in sleep you mock me." He reared back, ready to strike.

"Ahhhhhh!" A woman on the deck below let out an earth-shattering scream. Charlie had licked an ant off her foot and she'd woken up.

Nigel froze. His razor-sharp claws were a mere inch from Blu's feathery blue neck. But a moment's hesitation was a moment too long. A foghorn let out a deafening blast, and the sound was so loud it shook Gabi and Nigel off the roof. Nigel landed on a panicked

Charlie below. A crew member whacked them with an oar, sending them overboard. Charlie's tongue grabbed a life preserver in the nick of time.

"Wait for me!" Gabi cried, hopping to the railing. "Don't leave me!" She dove in after them.

Up on the roof, Tiago let out a scream in his sleep, startling Jewel awake.

"Tiago! Stop fooling around," she shushed.

"I didn't do anything!" he protested.

"Tiago Gunderson, listen to your mother," Blu mumbled, half asleep.

Tiago turned on his side and closed his eyes. "Awww, man."

None of them knew how close they'd just come to disaster.

✽ ✽ ✽ ✽ ✽

The next morning the sun was shining brightly over the Amazon. But while Blu and his family had had a mostly good night's sleep and were refreshed for the day ahead, Nigel, Gabi, and Charlie had spent the night clinging to the life preserver that dragged behind the boat.

The sound of Blu's voice caught Nigel's ear. There they were, flying into the distance, a blue blur against a blue sky. "They're getting away!" Nigel shrieked, slapping Charlie. "Wake up, you insect-eating idiot. Follow them!"

Charlie twisted his tongue into a corkscrew and used it in the water to propel them upriver.

"Better," Nigel snapped, shaking some water off his wings. "Now go ten times faster!"

Farther down the river, a base camp for a massive logging operation was being set up. A motorboat had pulled up to it, and a man dressed in a white suit, a white fedora, and expensive leather shoes alit onshore. He was the big boss of the camp and he did not look happy.

He walked into a tent where a group of loggers and a monkey were playing cards at a table. They were so engrossed in their game that they didn't notice him. But when he stabbed a knife in the table, they did.

"Having fun?" the boss asked as the monkey dropped his cards and scampered off. "Here's something fun." He threw a newspaper at the foreman. On the front page was a photo of Linda and Tulio under the headline *Rare Birds May Be Found?*

"If those tree huggers find their birds, they'll bring in the authorities," the boss said angrily. He ripped up the paper and stomped on it, furious. "And that will make me very, very unhappy!"

The loggers all looked at one another. No one dared breathe. No one wanted the boss to be unhappy.

The boss smoothed down the lapels of his suit and adjusted his hat. "I want those trees cut. Clear this area. *You don't want to see me unhappy, do you?*"

And with that, he walked past a map of the forest and out of the tent.

✿ ✿ ✿ ✿ ✿

Linda and Tulio had the same map pulled up on their tablet. And right now they were in the middle of studying it. It had been divided into quadrants. "Okay, we covered areas A and B. So I think we should continue with–" Linda thought out loud, tapping the map with her finger.

Tulio couldn't hear her. He had on headphones and was busy holding up a microphone to record bird sounds.

"Gwak! Gwak! Gwak!" he squawked into the forest, hoping to get a response back.

"Tulio, are you listening to me?" Linda asked, exasperated.

"You have reached your destination," intoned the GPS.

Blu looked at the others. "You see? It worked like a charm," he said proudly. "Here we are!"

"Uh . . . where?" Carla deadpanned. They were standing in the middle of an empty clearing.

Blu began pressing buttons. “Oh, these things have a margin of error.”

Jewel eyed the GPS. “I told you not to trust that woman.”

Meanwhile Bia and Tiago wandered off into the brush after a caterpillar.

“Oooh! That’s a Heliconius larva,” Bia said. “It feeds on rotting fruit.”

“Yeah, me too!” Tiago said as they disappeared from view.

“Hey kids! Kids! Stay close!” Blu called out.

“I’ll get them,” Jewel said, flying off.

“Okay, you guys stay put,” Blu told his friends. “Um, I’ll look around.”

“No worries, we’ll be here,” Rafael said, indicating Nico and Pedro. “We’re not going anywhere.”

But Nico and Pedro looked worried. “My feathers is poppin’ up on the back of my neck,” Pedro said.

“I don’t like this,” Nico said.

“Nuh-uh,” Pedro said with a shiver. “Let’s back it

up. *Beep. Beep. Beep.*" He mimicked the sound of a truck in reverse.

Blu flew off to a nearby tree. Pushing through some leaves, he gazed around. All he could see was thick jungle. "Come on, lady," he told the GPS. "Help me out here."

"Lost signal," the GPS beeped.

Blu groaned. "Great." He flew back to the clearing, but to his surprise, everyone was gone. "Okay . . . guys? Guys?" He fought back the instant panic that crept into his heart. "Ha, ha. Good one, guys. Very funny. Good, good. Very witty. Jewel? Where are you? Kids? Jewel?"

Suddenly, sharp talons burst out of the trees and grabbed him, carrying him off.

"Ahhhh!" Blu cried.

But no one was there to hear him.

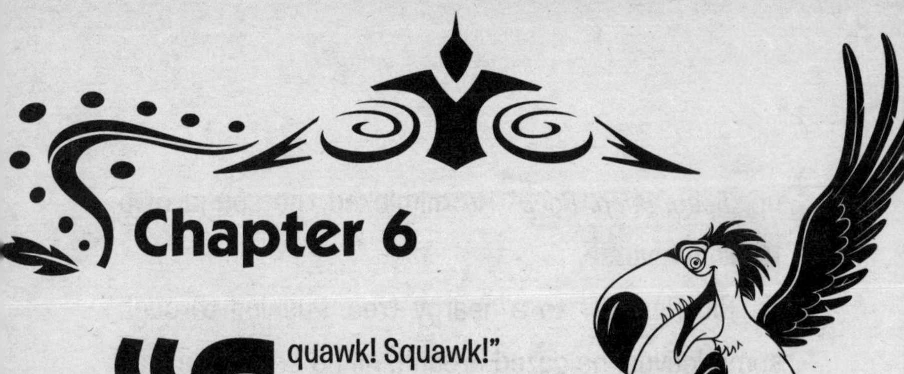

Chapter 6

"Squawk! Squawk!" The unmistakable sound of a rare blue Spix's Macaw rang out through the jungle.

"It's a macaw!" Tulio exclaimed. He and Linda took off after the sound. The bird kept squawking.

"Blu?" Linda shouted. She and Tulio pushed through thick jungle foliage and broke into a clearing. They were running so fast they almost didn't see the sheer cliff drop in front of them.

"I swear that sounded like Blu," she said, gasping for breath. She looked around but there were no macaws in sight. The trail had gone cold.

"That's impossible, Linda," Tulio panted. "He's back home in Rio, safe and sound."

✽ ✽ ✽ ✽ ✽

Blu continued to be dragged through the canopy of trees.

"I'm an American citizen, you savage!" he yelled, his feathers electrified with anger. "I demand to see my ambassador! I know my rights! I know my rights!"

Suddenly his captor dropped him, and Blu landed on top of a tree. He was surrounded by an intimidating pack of birds covered in camouflage.

Fumbling in his fanny pack, Blu whipped out his Adventure Knife and pushed a button. A spork popped out. Blu waved it wildly in front of him. "Back, you barbarian!"

The bird hesitated, staring at the spork with confusion.

"Yeah, that's right! It's a spoon *and* a fork!" Blu yelled. The bird flew away. "Be afraid!" Blu shouted. "Be very afraid!"

Someone tapped Blu on the shoulder and he whirled around, spork at the ready. "Whoa, whoa, whoa! Whoa, buddy. Put the spork down," a voice said.

To Blu's shock and relief, it was Rafael, and with him were Jewel and the kids.

"Let me go!" Nico's voice came from the sky. "Put me down! Hey, careful, that's my guitar talon." *Whish!* Nico and Pedro were dropped next to the others.

To everyone's surprise, one of the birds flew through a waterfall, revealing a bright blue feather. A little blue head popped out from behind some leaves. One by one, more blue heads started to peek out from branches, nests, and tree holes.

"I can't believe we found them!" Jewel said, awe-struck.

"Well, technically, they found us," Bia said as more macaws popped out. The macaws were very curious about the newcomers. "Okay, we're going to need some name tags," Blu said. A few of them circled Blu, touching his feathers and making him feel uncomfortable. One bird grabbed his mints from the fanny pack. "Whoa. Ah, hello. Okay, no . . . those are Tic Tacs. Not that you need one. But they're good. You eat them."

To his horror, the macaw threw the entire package of mints into its mouth and swallowed it whole.

"Oh, whoa, no, no, no, no, no!" Blu cried. "Not the whole box! Get that out of your mouth!" He grabbed the macaw and performed the Heimlich on him until he coughed the box up, right into the outstretched talons of Eduardo, the chief of the tribe.

"What is this doing here?" Eduardo bellowed, looking at the Tic Tacs and at Blu. "What is going on?"

The crowd quieted down. A macaw spoke up. "We found them flying too close to humans."

"Humans?" Eduardo yelled. "And who are you?"

"Uh . . ." Desperate to say the right thing, Blu backed up, searching for the words. Instead, he fell on his butt.

"'Uh' is not an appropriate answer." Eduardo got in Blu's face. "I asked you a question. Where did you come from?"

Jewel got in between them. "Hey!" she said,

jabbing her wing tip at Eduardo. "Back off!" She gave him a push that caught him off guard.

"Hey! Excuse me, young lady," Eduardo said.

Jewel stared into his eyes and gasped. Her expression softened. Could it be?

"I can't believe it," she said.

"How . . . how . . . how is this . . . ?" Eduardo started.

"I don't know," Jewel said, at a loss.

"I've looked everywhere for you!" Eduardo burst out.

Jewel rushed out the words. "When the humans came–"

"I had you under my wing and then you were–"

"Gone!" Jewel finished. "I'm here!" Jewel cried, rushing into his arms. "Daddy!"

Blu gaped at the sight of his wife and Eduardo embracing. "Daddy?"

"I missed you," Jewel cried.

"It's okay," Eduardo soothed. "It's okay now. Daddy has you."

Suddenly the birds were all aflutter. Everyone was hugging and laughing through tears of joy.

Eduardo pulled back to stare at Jewel. "Look at you. . . . It's my little girl, all grown up. You're so beautiful . . . just like your mother."

At the word "mother," Jewel looked hopefully into her father's eyes. The look he gave her back told her all she needed to know. Her mother was gone. Her head drooped in sadness as Eduardo hugged her close, stroking the back of her head.

"I am so sorry. I am so sorry I lost you. I can't imagine you alone this whole time," Eduardo told his daughter, holding her at wing's length.

Jewel took a big, gulping breath. "It's okay, Dad," she said. "I wasn't alone. Blu found me."

From the side, Blu shuffled nervously forward. His talons played uneasily with his fanny pack. He wanted to make a good impression. "Sure is nice to meet you, sir." He offered his father-in-law his wing.

But Eduardo wouldn't take it. "Tuck that wing away, Stu. "

Blu did as he was asked, afraid he had offended the chief.

"Now come here," Eduardo insisted, and Blu inched forward. "Closer."

"Oh, really . . ." This felt close enough to Blu.

"Closer," Eduardo urged. "You brought my Jewel back to me, I thank you." The two male birds were eye to eye. "I'm going to hug you now."

"Oh, uh, okay . . . should I just . . . ?" Blu awkwardly tried to hug Jewel's father when suddenly Eduardo embraced him.

"Now come here, Stu!"

Blu could hardly breathe as he tried to hug the older bird back. "Okay, there we are . . . my pleasure."

"Nico, you crying?" Pedro asked.

The little bird hiccupped. "It's a heavy moment and I'm very vulnerable right now."

Blu, Jewel, and their children—Carla, Bia, and Tiago—are the last known blue Spix's Macaws. They live in Rio with Linda, Tulio, and Fernando at Tulio's bird sanctuary.

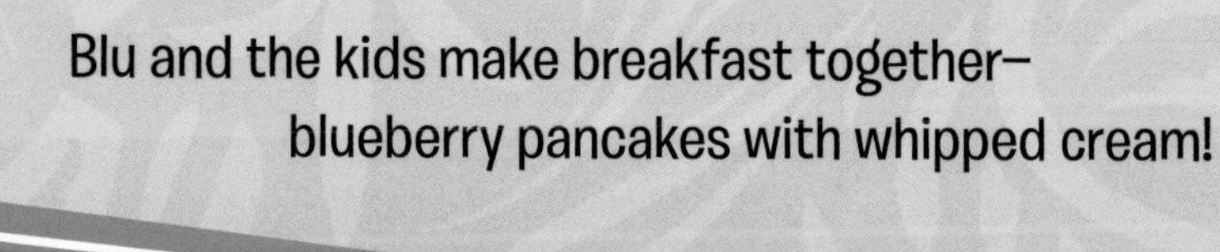

Blu and the kids make breakfast together—blueberry pancakes with whipped cream!

Jewel shows Blu a real Brazil nut—a rare find in the city!

Linda and Tulio make an important discovery in the Amazon jungle. There might be more blue Spix's Macaws!

Blu tells his friends that Jewel wants to go to the Amazon to find the other macaws. Rafael, Pedro, and Nico offer to go on the journey too.

Jewel is thrilled to be back in the wild. She can't wait to show her kids where she grew up.

Blu and Jewel give the kids a lift on the long journey.

Nigel, Gabi, and Charlie are eager to catch up to Blu and his family to start Nigel's plan for revenge.

The Amazon is filled with surprises! Blu and Jewel can't believe they've found a whole flock of blue macaws.

Jewel discovers her father, Eduardo, is the head of the blue macaw tribe.

Tiago, Bia, and Carla meet their grandfather.

The blue macaws lead Blu and Jewel to their hidden sanctuary in the Amazon where birds of blue feathers stick together.

"Come here, let me get you a hug," Pedro said, crying along with him.

Jewel wiped away a tear of joy as Bia flew to her. "Mom, are you okay?"

"Yeah, baby," Jewel said.

Eduardo's eyes widened. "'Mom'? I'm a grandpa? I'm a grandpa." He dropped Blu from the hug.

"Ow!" Blu yelped.

"Look at me!" Eduardo called out. "I'm a grandpa!"

"Daddy, this is Carla, Bia, and Tiago."

"Nice to meet you, sir," Bia said politely.

Eduardo chuckled. "There's no 'sir' around here, young lady. You will call me Pop-Pop." And he wrapped all three kids up in a hug.

"Pop-Pop! Oooh, I like that. It's got a nice ring to it!" Carla said.

Eduardo danced around with the kids, singing and laughing. "Kids, go easy on old Pop-Pop," Blu cautioned from the sidelines.

Eduardo stopped suddenly and turned to Blu.

"You can call me sir." Then he went back to hugging the children. "My daughter has returned!"

❀ ❀ ❀ ❀ ❀

The entire village of macaws came out to celebrate Jewel's return. Hundreds of them flew carefree in the lush, secluded cove they called home, surrounded by tall trees and beautiful waterfalls. The place was alive with happy energy.

Eduardo sat with Blu at the base of a tree as Jewel and the kids celebrated nearby.

A feisty old macaw made her way over to them. "Make way! Make way! Where is she? Where is my little niece?" the elderly macaw asked.

"Aunt Mimi!" Jewel exclaimed, hugging the sweet, eccentric macaw. "I missed you so much!"

"My little wildflower has returned! Finally there will be some fun back in the jungle," she said.

Eduardo leaned over to Blu. "I got to tell you when I first saw you, I thought, *Oh, boy, here comes one of those wimpy-winged birds.* But you're not." He paused.

"Right? Not you, Drew!" He punched him in the wing, almost knocking Blu over. "You're tough."

"Mimi, come here," Eduardo called. "I want you to meet Sue."

Mimi and Jewel walked over.

"Oooh, you snagged yourself a cute one," Aunt Mimi said.

"Actually, I'm *Blu*," he corrected politely.

"So am I, dear," Aunt Mimi said.

Blu tried to explain. "Oh, no, no, no–"

"We're all blue, dear. That's why they call us blue macaws." She turned to her niece. "Not too observant, is he?"

"Uh, no, really, that's my name," Blu said.

Jewel laughed. "Just go with it," she whispered to Blu. "Aunt Mimi, you haven't changed a bit!"

A strong breeze ruffled Blu's feathers, followed by someone singing in a soulful voice. Everyone in the jungle seemed to stop. Anticipation hung in the air. Blu joined the others and looked up to see a powerful-looking macaw soaring down to land. Blu didn't know who he was, but the bird was marvelous-looking: athletic and commanding, with a luscious head of feathers and the voice of a star.

"So that's what a blue macaw is supposed to look like," Pedro said, awestruck.

The majestic bird had only one focus: Jewel. He was singing directly to her–about how happy he was that she had returned, how amazing it was to see her again. He flew down to a branch near where a few female blue macaws sat. They swooned and fainted.

The bird glided down next to Jewel. "Welcome back, Jewel!"

"Roberto," Jewel said, blushing.

"Wow, you look great!" the dazzling macaw said.

"So do you!" Jewel said, smiling.

"We have so much catching up to do!"

Blu cleared his throat. "Uh, hey. Hi there. I'm Jewel's significant other." He was shocked when Roberto scooped him up and kissed him on both cheeks.

"Ahhh!" Roberto boomed. "So you're the lucky bird who swept Ju-Ju off her feet!"

Jewel giggled at the sound of her old nickname.

"Ju-Ju?" Blu repeated.

"Yeah, when we were kids we always had the cutest names for each other," Roberto explained.

"We did," Jewel said, giggling. "I called him Beto."

"That's adorable. I love doing the nicknames." Blu leaned toward Jewel. "You never mentioned any Roberto."

"There was nothing to mention," Jewel whispered back.

Eduardo joined them. "There's my wingman!" He grinned at Roberto. "Looking good, Roberto!"

"Look at you!" Roberto replied. He turned to Blu. "Eduardo taught me everything I know. He's the bird."

"No," Eduardo contradicted him. "You're the bird."

"You're the bird," Roberto insisted.

"You're the bird," Eduardo held firm.

Blu decided to join in. "Hey, how about you're both

the bird?" he said, trying to play along.

Eduardo and Roberto just looked at him. An awkward silence hung in the air. Thankfully, the music changed and Jewel's face lit up. "Oh wow, I remember this one!" she said.

"How could you forget?" Roberto said. "It's in our blood, baby! It's who we are." Roberto turned to Blu. "You don't mind if I borrow her for a minute, do you? I promise I'll bring her right back."

"Oh, well . . ." Actually Blu did mind. But Roberto had already swept Jewel onto the middle of the makeshift dance floor. Blu watched as the bird spun his wife expertly around. From the side, Nico, Pedro, and Carla bobbed to the beat.

"Come on, cutie!" Aunt Mimi said, taking Blu's wing. "Let's dance!" After a few seconds of spinning, Blu felt dizzy–and turned green. But Roberto and Jewel were on fire, singing and dancing together as if they'd never been apart. Everyone was watching them.

"Yo, this is untapped territory," Pedro said, shaking his feathers as he listened to them sing. "I am loving this sound!"

Eduardo brought Bia, Carla, and Tiago over, encouraging them to sing and dance too, and soon the whole tribe was singing. Blu tried his best to give it his all, but in the end, he found himself alone on the side, watching everyone else have fun.

"Come on, Dad!" Tiago urged, hopping around.

"Oh, that's okay," Blu assured him. "You guys have fun. I'm good."

Chapter 7

While the macaws were having a party, Nigel, Gabi, and Charlie were having a good dose of misery. They were hot. Sweaty. And uncomfortable. Especially Charlie. Nigel was perched on top of the anteater, and Gabi rode on top of Charlie's hat, fanning Nigel with a leaf. She hadn't stopped talking.

"You're the only one who knows what it feels like to be all alone. Misunderstood. You're the evil to my lethal."

Nigel shot her a look. "I can see why they call you Gabi." He glanced around. "Where are you, you filthy fowl?"

"Oh, I love watching you work," Gabi cooed.

Looking past Gabi, Nigel saw a group of blue birds

flying overhead.

"Halt!" he shouted. Charlie stopped short and Gabi was thrown off. "I've been going about this all wrong. I need to search from higher ground."

Nigel climbed down Charlie's head, not caring that he was stepping on his face. Puffing out his chest, he took a running start and jumped. *Bam!* He slammed hard into a tree. He tried it again. And again. But each time he failed, finally belly flopping unsuccessfully onto the ground.

"You stayed airborne for almost a full second that time!" Gabi said encouragingly. "Bravo! *Bravissimo!*"

Ignoring her, Nigel whipped around to face Charlie. "What are you looking at? Get me up there!"

Moments later, Nigel was standing on Charlie's head. Charlie used his tongue like a rope to scale the tree. "Higher! Higher . . . even higher!" Nigel commanded. "A little bit higher! Stop. Lower. Lower now. Yes! Perfect!" But when Nigel finally reached the perfect vantage point he was unhappy to see that

Blu and his family weren't alone. Instead, they were among hundreds of blue macaws.

"Ugh, it's an infestation. Keep celebrating," Nigel said to himself. "I'll be pooping on your party promptly."

Beneath him Charlie stretched to reach an ant, which caused him to lose his grip on the tree and slip. They all tumbled to the jungle floor.

Back at the macaw's village, the party was wrapping up. Nico and Pedro were very excited.

"We came to the right place!" Pedro enthused. "This is poppin'! It's poppin' in the Amazon!"

Nico nodded. "We can bring these macaws back to Rio and have the best Carnaval show ever! I am inspired!" He tossed his hat into the air but it didn't come back down.

Eduardo leaned over toward them. "Sorry to break it to you, city boys, but you'll have to find some other talent. Nobody leaves the tribe." In his talons was Nico's bottle-cap hat. "Oh, and no human things in the jungle. Understood?" He flew off holding the hat.

"What?" Pedro said, upset. "What's his problem?"

Nico slumped. "I feel naked."

"We coulda been legends," Pedro said, dejected. "I mean, we already are super mega dope, but you know what I'm saying?"

"We had it all," Nico picked up where Pedro had left off. "The undiscovered talent, the big idea. The inspiration. But if we can't bring these guys to Rio, we got nothing."

"Nothing? Hold your mangoes," Rafael said. "We still have Eva."

Nico and Pedro exchanged glances.

"What?" Rafael prompted.

Carla hurried over. "Guys, this jungle is huge. I bet we can find loads of untapped talent, if we just scout a little."

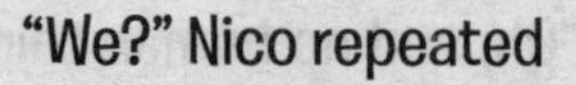

"We?" Nico repeated

"What you talkin' about, *we*?" Pedro said, frowning. "You speak French?"

Carla gave it to them straight. "No offense guys, but you're kinda old. And let's face it, I know the youth market."

Nico let out a low whistle. "Oooh, dude, you just got dissed," he told Pedro.

Pedro balked. "She was talking to you. I'm all youth. I swim in the fountain."

On the dance floor, Roberto and Jewel were finally taking a break. "Wow, you still got the moves, Ju-Ju," Roberto said as they flew over to Blu.

"Oh my gosh, I haven't danced like that in forever!" she gushed. "Seriously? When is the last time I had this much fun?"

"Um, New Year's, maybe?" Blu tried. "Just putting it out there."

Jewel wasn't picking up the hint. "Oh, I'm so exhausted."

"Yeah, we should get some rest," Blu spoke up. "Find a local inn or B and B nearby."

"Stop, stop, stop. What is this crazy talk?" Roberto cut in. "No, you guys are staying in my nest. I'm on patrol tonight. *Mi casa es su casa.*"

Jewel looked up at Roberto, obviously touched. "That's really nice, Beto."

"Thank you, but we're fine," Blu said, hating that plan. "Besides, our whole family couldn't possibly fit in your bachelor pad."

But it turned out that Roberto's "bachelor pad" was a palace.

"Whoa," Blu said, the word echoing in the cavernous space. He and Jewel stood in the atrium, gazing around Roberto's stylish, gigantic nest.

"Real estate must be pretty cheap around here," Blu mumbled.

"Wow," Jewel said, her eyes shining. "This is incredible."

Roberto played it down. "Oh, this old nest. It's

just something I put together last minute. With my own two wings, of course. And my strength. And my brawn. I'm into landscaping."

Tiago swooped in. "Dad, it's huge! It has six bedrooms! I get the big one!"

Carla swooped in next. "No! I'm the oldest."

"Only by three minutes, two point five seconds," Bia countered.

"I had hoped to one day be blessed with a flock of little Robertos to call my own," Roberto said by way of explanation. He smiled at Jewel, and Blu's eyes narrowed.

"I bet you did," he said thinly.

"No way!" Tiago shouted. "A birdbath! Yeah!" He slid down a branch into the water, splashing Blu.

Roberto put his wing around Blu. "Blu, let me tell you something. If anything, and I mean anything, ever happens to you, I will take care of your family." He smiled at all of them. "Sleep well." And then, as a clap of thunder sounded, he flew off.

❀ ❀ ❀ ❀ ❀

Outside Roberto's nest, rain fell in hard, noisy drops. Blu searched the nest for hidden dangers. "I'm not paranoid," he told himself. "I'm just practical." A shadow loomed over him and he whipped around. It was just a vine. "Ah, okay, all clear."

Jewel was singing a lullaby as she put the kids to bed. It made Blu feel a little better, hearing her soothing voice.

"Mom, sing it one more time, please," Tiago asked sleepily.

"Tomorrow, sweetie," Jewel told him. "Time for bed now."

After tucking the tired kids into bed, Blu and Jewel sat quietly together, looking out the window into the dark, wet rain forest.

"What an amazing day," Jewel said softly. "All this time, I never let myself hope they were still alive . . . but . . . but they are! We found our family, Blu!" She yawned. "This changes everything."

Blu had just dozed off, but Jewel's words startled him awake. *Changes everything?* What did she mean? "Yeah, wait, what? What's changing?"

But Jewel had fallen asleep.

Sighing, Blu stared down at his wife. What had he gotten himself into?

Chapter 8

Shafts of light made their way through the jungle canopy the next morning.

"C'mon, guys!" Carla said, waking Rafael, Nico, and Pedro up. "We have auditions."

The guys jolted awake. "Okay! I love it!" Rafael burst out, startled.

Carla sighed. "We haven't started yet. Here's the plan. We'll use our auditions today to pick the very best performers to take back to Rio. And Pop-Pop said tomorrow night we could put on a show right here to try it out!"

Nico held up his talons. "Whoa, kid. Slow down. It's early."

With a flourish, Carla stepped aside to reveal a crowd of animals that had already gathered.

Rafael let out a whistle. "Whooo, kid's been workin'!"

Carla grinned. "I told you I'd find talent! All right, hit it!"

The contestants lined up to do their thing. Everyone was hoping to secure a spot in the show.

A group of capybaras performed a synchronized swimming routine. They created a pyramid that rose out of the water. Fins circled around them. It was pretty amazing.

"Wow," Raphael said, impressed.

Things were going great until the surface of the water began to bubble and foam around the capybaras. When the bubbles stopped, all the animals were skeletons, except the one at the top of the pyramid.

"Ta-da!" the lone capybara cried.

Nico, Pedro, Rafael, and Carla looked at one another in horror.

"Is that a one-time thing?" Rafael asked. "Or are there more of you?"

Carla took a breath. "Well, we have more to go through. Next!"

The acts kept coming. There was a sloth that woke up to sing and fell promptly back to sleep when she finished. Next, two turtles demonstrated a capoeira routine in slow motion. Nothing was exciting the judges.

The next contestant, a baby capybara, stepped into the spotlight. "Hi, my name is Clara the Capybara. And I will be singing my favorite song." She began to sing "Memory," her voice light and sweet.

The judges agreed she was doing a wonderful job. But to their horror, a jaguar sprang out of the jungle and chomped the capybara down in one bite. The capybara continued to sing *inside* the jaguar. The jaguar lip-synced along.

"If they keep eating each other, we got no show," Nico muttered.

Carla sighed. "Okay, we'll just keep looking."

When Blu woke up, a spider was sitting on his face. "Ahhh!" he cried. Tiago laughed–he'd been holding the spider on the end of a string while a group of macaw kids watched and laughed.

"Tiago!" Blu scolded.

Jewel flew past, joining Tiago. "Good morning, sweetie! C'mon, Blu, join us! Tiago, I'll race ya! Last one to the waterfall is a rotten egg!"

Blu watched as they did loop de loops and barrel rolls, then slid down a waterfall.

"Yeah!" Tiago shouted. "This is great!"

Jewel landed on a branch. "Tiago!" she called, tossing him a piece of fruit. She ripped into her own fruit, juice dripping down her beak.

Blu had never seen her act this way. "Whoa."

He decided to go brush his teeth first, keeping up his regular routine. But as he was brushing, he realized he wasn't alone. Eduardo was standing there. Watching him.

"Morning!" Eduardo bellowed.

Blu swallowed down the toothpaste foam and started coughing. He didn't like being snuck up on.

"See you overslept a little bit here, son," Eduardo said. "Our days start pretty early here in the jungle."

Jewel swept back in and Blu quickly wiped his beak.

"Morning, Daddy!"

"That's my girl, already up and at 'em!" Eduardo said proudly.

"Why did you let me sleep in?" Blu asked Jewel under his breath. He hated looking lazy in front of his father-in-law.

Jewel looked at him. "What are you talking about? You sleep in every day!"

"Yeah, but-"

Bia swooped in carrying clay in her talons. "Hey, Dad, Aunt Mimi says clay is good for your digestion. Try some!" And despite Blu's protests, Bia shoved the clay into his beak, making him cough again.

"It's good, right?" Bia grinned. "I'm gonna go get some more." She took off.

"Smart girl. Clearly she takes after her mother," Eduardo said fondly. "So I thought I'd take Stu here for a little tour of the area. Show him around." He put his arm around Blu. "Let's shake that city off you, son."

"Oh, that's a great idea!" Jewel exclaimed. "You go have fun with Daddy and I'll explore around here with the kids!"

"Oh, oh yeah, okay. Sure. Yeah, great, I just gotta–" Blu pulled out his fanny pack. "Okay, ready."

Eduardo cleared his throat. "Okay. Stu, come here. It's okay, Stu. Come closer."

Blu moved a little closer. "Even more? Okay, yeah."

"Not so close," Eduardo said.

Blu backed off. "Oh, okay."

Eduardo sighed. "Listen, I know you come from a . . . I realize a different background." He pointed to the pack. "But, you gotta . . . you gotta lose that human pocket, okay?"

"Oh, this is a fanny pack," Blu corrected.

"It's human," Eduardo said firmly. "And I can't have my flock corrupted, so you understand." Finished, Eduardo flew off. "I'll meet you by the clay banks!" he called.

"Come on . . . corrupted?" Blu let out, exasperated. "By a fanny pack?"

Jewel tried to calm him. "Remember how I was when I met you?"

Blu nodded. "Uh, yeah. Rude, violent, borderline psychotic."

Jewel smiled. "All right, easy there, partner. I was wild. These are wild birds." She smoothed Blu's feathers. "We have to try to be culturally sensitive while we're here. Besides, it won't kill you to leave behind the fanny pack."

"All right," Blu agreed. Jewel flew off as Blu put the pack on the ground.

"Happy wife, happy life," he said, sighing. He took flight, trying to keep up. Then he looked back at Jewel, with the kids and Roberto.

Jewel waved. "Have fun, honey!"

"Uh, yeah, sure. Bye!"

✿ ✿ ✿ ✿ ✿

In another part of the jungle, a different expedition was taking place. Nigel, Gabi, and Charlie stalked through the rain forest. Nigel had disguised himself with leaves and vines.

"There he is," Nigel said, looking into the sky. A blue bird was flying unsteadily ahead of them. "Now's our chance. Prepare the tongue-a-pult." He positioned himself in the center of Charlie's outstretched tongue, which was being used as a slingshot.

"Charlie, make me fly again!" Nigel shrieked. Charlie launched him forward like a missile. He flew through the air, talons extended like a hawk going in for the kill.

"Bow before the conquering cockatoo!" he screamed, tackling the bird midair and pinning it by the throat.

But it wasn't Blu. It was a blue-and-gold macaw

named Peri. "Dude, what's your problem?" Peri yelped, scared.

Nigel had been so sure. . . .

"Bird, that was sick! Now that's the energy you bring to an audition." Confused, Nigel looked around to find the source of the voice. He'd stumbled right into what looked like an audition. He recognized Nico, Pedro, and Carla. A line of jungle animals waited on a large flat rock in front of a waterfall.

Nigel blinked. "Audition?"

Peri got up. "Yeah, that's actually why I'm here. I've got a great little num–"

Nigel punted the macaw and then turned to Nico and Pedro. "Go on."

"We're looking for a new star!" Nico said.

Nigel's ears pricked up. "Star?"

Rafael was peering at him. "You look familiar. Don't I know you from somewhere?"

"No, no. I don't think so," Nigel lied. "Ummm . . . no. I'm, ummm, Bob. Yes, Bob the bird."

"Catchy name!" Carla said.

Pedro tilted his head. "Okay, Bob, whatever, show us what you got!"

Nigel thought for a minute. Then he began to sing the words to a disco song he knew, putting his own spin on it. Warming up as he went along, he began kicking the other contestants out of line as he sang.

Everyone got into the performance and when the song ended, there was wild applause.

"Yes! Thank you! I've been Bob the bird."

"He is so hot!" Gabi whispered.

Pedro was grinning. "Boom! That's it! You in!"

"Okay, you're good, I'll give you that." Rafael shrugged. "I mean, he's no Eva."

"We'll see you at the performance tomorrow night," Nico told him.

Carla beamed. "Everyone from the village is coming. It's gonna be off the charts!"

"Everyone?" Nigel inquired, feeling his excitement grow. He would see his plan through after all.

✿ ✿ ✿ ✿ ✿

"It's the perfect plan," Nigel said to Gabi later. He kept plucking quills out of the porcupine that was hung upside down in front of him, looking for the sharpest one. "Be happy we're only plucking you, porcupine."

"Ow!" the little porcupine cried in protest.

"Instead of chasing that bird all over the jungle, we let him come to us, at the Carnaval show." Nigel found a quill that met his standards. "I'll mesmerize them from the stage. While in the audience, you, my little Gabi, you will be my petite weapon of mass destruction!"

Nigel rubbed the quill up Gabi's back, coating it with her poison. She gave an excited shudder. Then he placed the quill into the end of Charlie's nose and aimed him at his target. "It will be a performance to die for!"

Charlie shot the quill. It flew toward its target—a combination of fruit and leaves made to look like Blu.

Bull's-eye! Nigel cackled and Gabi joined in.

"It only works when I do it," Nigel snapped, shutting Gabi up.

Carnaval couldn't happen soon enough.

Chapter 9

"Oooh, hey. You are fast. You are really, really fast. I think I pulled a wing or something," Blu said, flying behind Eduardo. He was struggling to keep up. "You are really fast for an old bird."

Eduardo shot him a look.

Blu gulped, but continued. "For such a wise . . . wise bird. *Wise* is what I meant to say. Wise bird. Which sometimes comes with age, but also can happen when you're young like you, in your case." He continued talking to try to undo what he'd just said. "You can be wise and young. Which is kind of a rare combination but thrilling when it happens."

"Be quiet!" Eduardo ordered. "Listen to me, son. You have my family to watch over and you're . . . soft. You need to learn the basics of jungle survival. Patrol, provide, protect. You need training."

Suddenly Eduardo barrel rolled into a nosedive as

Blu watched, confused.

"Training?" Blu repeated. "I thought we were sightseeing."

A few minutes later, Blu found himself lying in a mud puddle as Eduardo, camouflaged in mud, stood over him like a drill sergeant.

"Be one with the mud!" Eduardo barked. Blu started rolling around, not sure what to do.

"Feel it! Live it! Put that mud everywhere!"

Trying to please Eduardo, Blu started throwing mud on himself. But it got in his mouth, causing him to choke.

"Roll around! Roll around! Move it!" Eduardo continued.

Next, Eduardo took Blu deep in the jungle and had him hang upside down on vines. "You are alone in the jungle," Eduardo told him, setting the scene. "You get caught in a trap. You hear that?"

"No," Blu whimpered.

Eduardo's eyes widened. "It's the jaguars fast

approaching! What do you do?"

Blu thought hard. "Well, if I had my fanny pack—"

"You use your beak!" Eduardo burst out. "Your beak is your most important tool!"

"Okay, use my beak," Blu repeated. He tried to reach up and use his beak to cut the vine, but he couldn't do it. "I . . . almost . . ."

"Time's up," Eduardo said, sounding disgusted. "You're jaguar meat." He reached up and snipped the vine with his beak and Blu landed hard on the ground. "Roberto got it on the first try," he told him.

Blu groaned. Of course he did.

The torture continued. Eduardo had Blu jump across a row of alligator snouts like a football player running through tires. "Come on!" Eduardo screamed at him. "You don't want to be eaten! Faster! Faster! Faster!"

Then they moved on to flying. Blu, his feathers covered with dried mud and while holding sticks, tried to keep up with Eduardo flying over the river.

"Up . . . up . . . and hover! Hover! Now, backwards!"

"Backwards?" Blu screeched. "Only hummingbirds can fly backwards!" As he said this, Eduardo flew past him, backward.

"Backwards!" Eduardo shouted. Blu flapped his wings in all directions to no avail.

The river was next. Some pink river dolphins surfaced, chattering. They chirped something to Eduardo and he chirped back. "Under, over, under, over," he told Blu, who weaved under the dolphins. "Higher! Lower! Good job!"

"Oh, thanks," Blu said, relieved.

"Not you," Eduardo said before high-fiving one of the dolphins.

Finally they took a break. Eduardo and Blu sat on top of a majestic tree in the middle of a Brazil nut grove.

"The beauty–this whole grove is Brazil nut trees," Eduardo said, closing his eyes and breathing deeply. "Our most prized crop. The trees feed us. Sustain us.

We honor and protect all the nature around us, great and small."

Blu's eyelids drooped. "Wake up!" Eduardo snapped.

"I'm up! I'm up!" Blu said, startled.

Eduardo caught a flower that had fallen off the tree. "From this tiny flower comes a seed. A seed that becomes the mightiest tree that shelters and nourishes us all." He tossed Blu a nut, and then opened one for himself and ate it.

"I could use a snack," Blu said, trying to bite into the nut. The nut jammed inside his mouth.

Some red macaws were watching them from the other side of the river. "Yo, Eddie!" one of them called. His name was Felipe. "Who's your sidekick? You got a nurse now?" The red macaws laughed.

"Imphhp Bluph," Blu said, trying to introduce himself.

"Never mind him," Eduardo retorted. "Aren't you boys getting a little too close to our side?"

Felipe grinned. "Your grove is looking mighty fine."

"Yeah, and you boys better stay out of it," Eduardo warned.

Felipe spread his wings. "Hey, relax. You know we got nothing but mad love for you." The red macaws all laughed, and then followed Felipe as he flew away.

"They seem nice," Blu said sarcastically.

"They have their side and we have ours. And it's going to stay that way as long as I'm in charge," Eduardo told him.

A sound came from the brush nearby.

"Shhh," Eduardo warned. He tensed as the cracking sound grew closer–and then they heard a bird squawk. The sound grew louder. Below them, Linda and Tulio were moving slowly through the brush. Tulio was making squawking sounds into a microphone.

"Lin–" Blu began before Eduardo clapped his wing over Blu's beak.

Linda looked up, searching the trees. Then she and Tulio moved on.

"What are you doing?" Blu said when Eduardo removed his wing.

"Are you out of your mind? They're humans!" Eduardo hissed.

"That's Linda!" Blu cried.

Eduardo looked puzzled. "What's a linda?"

Blu groaned. "She raised me."

"What?" Eduardo looked stricken. "You were a *pet*?"

"No, no, no," Blu clarified. "I mean, it wasn't like that. I was a companion.

"You liked it?" Eduardo asked, incredulous. "That explains everything."

"Linda is family," Blu said firmly.

The elder bird got in his face. "Family is family."

Blu was fed up. "Eduardo, they are good people!"

Eduardo moved so his eyeballs were millimeters from Blu's. "There are no good people! Listen to me very carefully, either you're with us or you're against us. Understood?"

Blu gulped. "Yeah, got it."

"Good."

❀ ❀ ❀ ❀ ❀

When Blu and Eduardo returned to the village, Blu was feeling pretty low. He was tired, muddy, and still had a few branches stuck to his feathers.

"Blu! You're back!" Jewel said, flying over to him. "Was it fun?"

"Oh, we had a great time!" Eduardo said smoothly.

Tiago came over. "Dad, Uncle Beto showed me some cool flying tricks!"

"Uncle?" Blu repeated warily.

"Look!" Tiago exclaimed. "I can fly backwards!" And he did.

"You're a natural, T-Bird," Roberto praised him. He and Tiago did a head butt and wing bump.

Eduardo looked on proudly. "You've got your mother's genes. It's never too soon to learn the ways of the jungle, Tiago." He shot Blu a look. "Although some may never learn."

Blu let out a tired sigh. "I'm gonna go clean up." He flew off.

"We saw humans," Eduardo told Roberto.

"Humans!" Roberto repeated, nervous.

"Calm yourself. I don't want that bird leaving the village," Eduardo said, looking at Blu in the distance. "Keep an eye on him."

Chapter 10

Away from the group, Blu opened his fanny pack. Inside was the Tic Tac box. He popped a few in his mouth. "So minty." He rummaged around the pack until he found the GPS. He tried again to punch in Linda and Tulio's campsite coordinates. *Bzzz. Bzzz.* A mosquito buzzed around him. Blu tried to swat it. He missed. He tried again. And missed.

Ping!

"Yes!" Blu cheered as the GPS found its signal. He reached into his pack, grabbed his bug spray, and sprayed it into the air, trying to get the mosquito. Instead, he sprayed himself in the eyes.

"Hey, sweetie, there you are!" It was Jewel. "Come on, the whole tribe is gathering for sunset."

"Wait, wait! You know, we saw Linda and Tulio

today!" he told her, holding up the GPS. "And I just found the location of their camp! We have to go get them and bring them here!"

Jewel didn't look so sure. "I don't know, Blu."

What did she mean, she didn't know? he wondered.

"What's to know? That was our plan all along, right? To help them find this place," Blu reminded her.

"Maybe some places shouldn't be found," Jewel told him. "Maybe they should just be left alone."

Blu looked at her, not sure where she was going with this. The mosquito began to buzz again. Blu's head bobbed and his eyes crossed as he tried to follow it.

Jewel found it first. She snagged it right out of the air and gulped it down.

Blu stared, aghast. What had gotten into her? Jewel was taking this wild thing a little too far.

❀ ❀ ❀ ❀ ❀

Blu was freaking out to his friends. "She ate a bug!" he exclaimed to Rafael later that night. "A bug!"

"Blu, Blu, Blu. Calm down," his friend urged.

Blu paced back and forth. "Oh! Oh! And her father? Total nut job. He's got this weird thing about humans. . . ."

In another part of the macaw village, Eduardo was venting to Aunt Mimi. "He's got this weird thing about humans!" Eduardo said, shaking his head.

"I like him," Aunt Mimi declared. "And so does Jewel."

Eduardo wasn't having it. "How can he protect her? He's not strong enough."

Aunt Mimi sighed. "Eduardo, give him a chance."

"A chance?" Eduardo repeated, incredulous. "How can I trust a bird that's a pet? He is a liability and he doesn't belong here."

Blu continued to panic. "I don't even belong here," he said, animatedly throwing up his wings. "I thought we were going on a little vacation. We'd help Linda and Tulio find the flock and then head home."

✽ ✽ ✽ ✽ ✽

"I'm not even sure he's a bird," Eduardo ranted, only half joking.

"But he makes our Jewel really happy," Aunt Mimi pointed out.

Eduardo knew it was true. But still . . . "I just don't want anything to happen to her. Mimi, I–"

✽ ✽ ✽ ✽ ✽

"I can't lose her!" Blu cried.

Rafael did his best to calm him down. "She's wild about you, Blu. But she's also wild about the wild."

"Which means, you gotta go native!" Pedro announced.

"Yeah, you gotta bird up!" Nico encouraged him.

Blu was confused. "Bird up?" What did that even mean?

Nico tried to explain. "You gotta give yourself over to this place, man. See it like she sees it!"

"Feel the rhythms she feels," Pedro said.

"Taste the flavors she's tastin'!" Nico added.

Blu thought for a moment. "So I should . . . eat a bug?"

Nico and Pedro recoiled in horror. "Uh, no," Pedro said quickly. "That's just nasty."

Just then Carla arrived. She hurried over to them. "Guys, what are you doing? We've gotta get ready for tomorrow. Come on! Chop-chop!"

Pedro gave her an appraising stare. "Wow, she puts the business in show business."

"Dad, you're coming to the show tomorrow night, right?" Carla asked Blu. "It's gonna be awesome!"

Blu nodded. "Yeah, sure, wouldn't miss it!"

Carla smiled. "Great. Now, no offense, but we need the stage."

"You got it," Blu told her. As he left, he accidentally bumped into someone. Nigel.

"Oh, sorry," the cockatoo said, distracted.

"Sorry. Sorry," Blu replied.

"Excuse me." Nigel pushed past him, hurrying to rehearsal.

"No problem," Blu replied, walking away.

❀ ❀ ❀ ❀ ❀

On the makeshift stage, Charlie was practicing some dance moves. Nigel wasn't having it. "No. Stop. Stop. Stop. Cut! Cut! Stop!" He grew more exasperated with each second. He stormed onstage. "Glitter! Where is my glitter? Glitter is absolutely essential for a magical performance. Do you know nothing?" he shouted. "Ugh, it's absolutely heartbreaking to see brilliant choreography being butchered. If we want this plan to work, you have to be perfect!"

Nigel showed Charlie the steps once more. "It's spin, right, grapevine left, and then, with you stage left, I will do my flourish–ta da!–and Gabi, that will be the cue for you to do the deadly deed."

Gabi let out a sigh. "Oh, Nigel. You are the maestro of mayhem."

Suddenly, Nigel stopped short. Something was missing.

Charlie dutifully went off in search of glitter. Gabi gazed at Nigel, lovestruck. "Did that Shakespeare guy ever write anything about a pair of star-crossed lovers separated by a fate beyond their control?" she asked softly.

"*Romeo and Juliet*," Nigel snapped, getting back into the rehearsal. "A tragedy. Both of them die in the end. It was a poisonous love."

Gabi thought that was the most romantic thing she'd ever heard.

Chapter 11

It was another beautiful, sunny day in the rain forest. Jewel zoomed in, her feathers ruffling in the morning breeze. "Woo-hoooo!" she cried, blasting past the nest and landing on a nearby branch. "What a glorious morning! I forgot I could have mornings like this."

Roberto landed nearby, carrying a large branch full of Brazil nut pods. "Your favorite," he told her, handing her a large nut.

"You remembered!" Jewel squealed. "Isn't that nice?" She yanked a nut off the branch with her claws and tore into it. "Oh, it's so crazy good! Thank you so much, Roberto!"

Roberto smiled down at her. "Not at all. And may I say, you look lovely this morning."

Jewel flushed. "Oh, stop it, Beto." They leaned in for a kiss.

"Yeah," Blu said, seething. "You heard her. Stop it!"

And it was at that moment that Blu jolted awake. His brow was covered with sweat. Jewel, Roberto, kissing . . . it had only been a nightmare. Jewel and the kids were still fast asleep.

Shaking off the horrible dream, Blu crept silently past his family and reached for his fanny pack. *Click!* He slid the buckle in place, relieved that the sound didn't wake Jewel up. Then he snuck out of the nest and flew off.

"*I'll* be the one to surprise her," he told himself, filled with determination. "Breakfast in bed, coming up!"

✽ ✽ ✽ ✽ ✽

Linda and Tulio continued to search for more Spix's Macaws. They had climbed up in a tree for a better vantage point, when a bunch of bats flew out of a hole in the tree, startling Tulio. He lost his grip and suddenly found himself dangling from the ropes.

"Tulio!" Linda cried. "Tulio, are you okay?"

"I'm fine," Tulio told her. "I'm okay."

But something wasn't okay. In the distance they could make out smoke. They hurried to investigate. A long double row of trees was marked with red X's spray painted on them. In between the rows, the underbrush had been cut and slashed, leaving an ugly gaping hole in the greenery. A chain saw was roaring nearby.

"Tulio, they're cutting down the forest," Linda whispered, her voice shaking with rage. She pushed past him, toward the loggers.

"Linda!" Tulio exclaimed. "Where are you going?"

Linda kept moving. "To talk to them. You talk to birds, I talk to humans."

"No, wait! Don't!" Tulio pleaded.

Linda stepped up behind a huge man using a chain saw. "Hey! Hey, mister!" she said, jabbing him with her finger. "Hellooooo?"

The logger spun around, almost hitting her with the saw. "You take it easy with that chain saw," she told him. "There are rare birds living around here. You can't cut down those trees."

The man just stared at Linda.

"Oooh, sweetheart!" Tulio said, running up to them. "There you are! I was looking for you." He turned to the logger. "Beautiful out here, isn't it?" He smiled broadly.

"You two lost?" came a voice. It was the foreman.

"Lost? No, no, hahaha, lost. Ah, we're here on our honeymoon," Tulio said, forcing a chuckle. "We're actually just heading back to join the tour." He tugged on Linda's arm. "Come along, dear. Let's go. Let's go. We're late."

The foreman was still studying them as Tulio dragged Linda away. "Linda, logs aren't the only things these guys cut," he said as they left.

"Let's see how tough they act when we call the authorities!" she fumed.

Tulio pulled her along, but he kept looking back

over his shoulder. He had the sneaking suspicion they were being followed.

❀ ❀ ❀ ❀ ❀

Blu flew back and forth, looking for a Brazil nut tree. "Where are those things?" he said, landing on a branch. "I know they're around here somewhere."

A hand reached out of the leaves and tapped him on the shoulder. Blu spun around. No one was there. But then another hand grabbed his tail.

Click! A hand grabbed his fanny pack. Monkeys! They took off running across the branches.

"Hey!" Blu cried angrily. "Hey, hey! No, hey! Hey! Come back here!" Blu chased the monkeys through the jungle, desperate to get his stuff back. Now the monkeys were rifling through his fanny pack. His stuff was spilling out. One monkey grabbed the GPS.

"Hey, no! Stop it!" Blu shouted. The monkey tossed the GPS. "No, no! Be careful with that!" Blu lunged forward, catching it just in time.

Another monkey took out Blu's electric toothbrush.

"No! No! Don't do it!" Blu pleaded, horrified to see the monkey shove the brush in his ear. "Ewwww!"

Monkeys were looping Blu's roll of toilet paper all over the branches. "Stop it!" he yelled. Not watching where he was going, Blu flew deeper into the jungle.

He spotted one of the monkeys sitting on a branch, inspecting the fanny pack. Blu reached over and snatched it back. "Gotcha!" He was breathing hard. "Thank you," he said sarcastically.

Blu looked around. He was in a huge Brazil nut tree grove. "Finally, Brazil nuts," he said. He landed on a branch, opened his fanny pack, and pulled out his Adventurer's Knife. "*This* is my most important tool," he declared. He slid up the can-opener apparatus and used it to try to pry a nut loose. It didn't work. So he tried the corkscrew and then the set of pliers. Nothing.

"Ugh, everything but a knife," he said, frustrated. He tossed the knife back into his fanny pack and attacked the nut with his talons. Then he tried to pull a nut pod off the tree with his beak. Despite some serious tugging, it was on there tight.

"Well, well, well. What do we have here?"

Blu looked up to see Felipe landing nearby with his gang of red macaws. They were all smiling widely at him. Too widely.

This made Blu nervous. He clutched the branch.

"I guess old Eddie's rules don't apply to everyone," Felipe said, squinting at him. "You're on *our* side."

"Oh, oh really? Okay. My bad," Blu apologized, gulping. "I didn't know that." He let go of the branch and it snapped forward, launching the nut pod into the air and smacking the red macaw in the face.

"Oh! Oops!" Blu cried. "Sorry! Sorry!"

The red macaw rubbed his beak where the nut pod had hit him. "You come over here, you take our food, and now you insult me," he said with a steely glare.

"Oh, oh, no, no, no," Blu squeaked out. "This is all just a big misunderstanding."

"You know, I wish I could accept your apology. You

seem like a nice bird," the red macaw said coldly. "But this means war."

"What?" Blu was aghast. "Does it have to? Can it mean something else?"

Felipe's eyes narrowed. "Today. In the pit of doom."

Blu let out a nervous giggle. "Sorry. The pit of doom? Really?"

"Yeah."

"Oh, really," Blu said, swallowing.

"High noon. Oh, I'll make some room. Sweep you up like a broom." Then Felipe and his gang took off, laughing.

What have I done? Blu wondered, watching them fly away.

✿ ✿ ✿ ✿ ✿

"You did what?" Eduardo yelled again. His feathers stood on edge and his voice trembled with anger.

"It was an accident," Blu tried to explain for the third time. His father-in-law was definitely furious.

Things were not looking–or feeling–good.

Jewel flew in and took in the tense scene. "Hey, whoa, what's going on?"

Eduardo snorted. "Thanks to Stu here, we're going to have to battle for the foraging rights to the entire grove!" He threw up his wings in disgust.

"I was just trying to get a nut!" Blu told Jewel. "One nut!"

"You don't even like nuts," Jewel said, staring at him. "What's gotten into you, Blu?"

"I was getting it for you!" Blu burst out, frustrated.

Jewel's eyes softened. "Oh, you were?"

"Roberto, get your best birds on this," Eduardo said, resigned. "It's gonna be brutal."

Roberto nodded. "I'm on it."

Eduardo looked at Blu. "All right, you stay behind, we'll deal with this."

"Wait–" Blu said.

"Blu, he's right," Jewel said. "Maybe you should let Dad and Roberto handle it."

Didn't Jewel believe in him? "You don't think I can do this," he said flatly.

She hesitated. "No, I-I just don't know if it's your area of expertise."

A huge mass of blue macaws had gathered along a deep Amazonian gorge. Across from them were an equal number of red macaws. The blue macaws, led by Roberto, were chanting and thumping their feet in what looked like a primal war dance. They looked like armies preparing for battle.

"This is ridiculous!" Blu told Eduardo. "We can share the grove."

"You brought this on us," Eduardo told him. "Now watch."

Roberto faced off against Felipe in the middle of the arena. The tension was building.

A referee bird placed a Brazil nut in between them. Roberto grabbed the nut and kicked it to another blue macaw, who in turn head butted it toward the goal. The red goalie made the save.

"Push up!" the red goalie yelled, punting the nut back into play.

It dawned on Blu what was going on. This wasn't a duel to the death. It was a game. Air soccer! "It's a game? It's only a game," he said, relieved.

"It's not a game, it's war," Eduardo boomed.

"It's like air soccer!" Blu exclaimed. "I can do this! Like Pele, Ronaldinho, or Neymar! I watch those guys on TV all the time! Ha ha!" He turned to Eduardo. "So what position do I play?"

Eduardo's eyes were slits. "Actually, I do have the perfect spot for you."

The perfect spot turned out to be the bench. Blu sat there, miserable, wedged between some loser birds, watching as Roberto made cool move after cool move.

"Goallllll!" Tiago shouted when Roberto scored. The blue macaws went wild, tackling Roberto.

"Show-off," Blu muttered. He flew off the bench

and along the side of the stadium, starting the wave.

The referee tossed another nut into play. Blue and red feathers were flying as both teams went after the ball. The reds got it and went for the goal. Score! Now the game was tied.

The game was fast and furious. Roberto managed to get the nut and scored again. Now it was 2 to 1.

"I could have done that," Blu said as everyone congratulated Roberto.

Eduardo heard him. "You're in!" he shouted.

Blu pointed to himself. "Really?"

"Not you," Eduardo said. "You!" Blu watched as the old decrepit macaw Eduardo had actually been pointing to limped out onto the field.

"Watch and learn," the old macaw said, and then promptly injured himself.

Eduardo stared at Blu. He was out of options. "All right, get in there."

"Yes!" Blu shouted, flying out to join the others.

"Yeah, Dad!" Bia yelled. Blu looked back to see his

kids cheering him on. It felt good.

The referee launched a new nut. Blu joined the others in diving for it, sending the crowd into a frenzy.

Blue macaws passed the pod back and forth over Blu's head. "I'm open! I'm open! Toss it to me! Pass to me, I'm open!" he screamed. "Pass the ball to me!"

Roberto kicked the ball to Blu. But it bounced off his face–and into the talons of a red macaw, who scored. Now it was 2 to 2.

When the next nut was launched, all the birds raced for it.

"Go get it, Dad!" Tiago shouted.

"One more, Blu!" Rafael urged.

"Come on, Blu," Jewel called out. Just before the pod hit the water, Blu grabbed it. He zipped along the water, dodging jumping piranhas who were snapping at the nut.

"Blu! Blu! Blu!" his friends were chanting. He did some fancy footwork and the crowd went even wilder.

"Pass the ball!" Eduardo bellowed. "Pass the ball!"

Instead, Blu kicked the nut around with some awesome moves, dodging red macaws flying at him from every direction. Feeling confident, he flew past Eduardo.

"Pass the ball!" Eduardo screamed again.

Wham! Two red macaws smacked into Blu, spinning him around. When he righted himself, he flew back in the other direction.

Blu got closer to the goal. This was it. He did a bicycle kick. A red macaw flew out of his way, revealing the blue macaw goalie trying to wave him off. But it was too late. The nut was flying into the goal.

Blu threw his wings up in victory. But the crowd was silent. No one was cheering with him. The ref threw a red berry on the scoreboard. Blu's wings dropped. Blu had scored a goal . . . for the other team.

As the blue macaws gave Blu dirty looks, the red macaws laughed and cheered.

"Thanks for the goal, Blu," Felipe said, patting him

on the back. "Couldn't have done it without you."

"Oh, and Eduardo?" Felipe said as the elder bird flew over, obviously annoyed. "From now on, stay out of our grove." He flew off with the laughing red macaws.

Eduardo gave Blu a dark look. "I shouldn't have expected more from a human's pet."

Blu looked into the crowd. It was a sea of disappointment. Blu had let everyone–especially his family–down.

Chapter 12

A short while later, Blu sat glumly on a branch. He hung his head when Jewel approached.

"Hey, it'll be all right," Jewel said softly.

"I think it's time we headed home," Blu said morosely.

"The kids are thriving," Jewel told him. "They love being in the wild."

"What are you saying?" Blu asked.

Jewel didn't say anything at first. "Blu, maybe this place is home."

"*What?*" Blu blurted out. "We already have a great home in Rio!"

"I know it hasn't been easy for you to adjust here–" Jewel began.

"I've been trying so hard, Jewel, but I don't belong in the jungle. I can't do this anymore." He could feel his heart beating double-time.

Jewel took a breath. "Maybe you just need to give it more time. Daddy and Roberto can help you–"

"Roberto!" Blu was fed up. "Enough with this guy! Oh, and P.S., your father hates me! Trust me, your family would be very happy if I left."

Jewel was stung. "Whoa, whoa, whoa. My family is your family."

"Your dad doesn't even know who I am," Blu snapped. "Stu, Drew, Lou, or Sue, I'll never be 'the bird,' like Roberto!"

"Oh, I see what this is about," Jewel bit back. "Maybe you need to open your eyes and think about us instead of just yourself. " She stormed off.

Linda and Tulio were on a mission as they moved quickly through the jungle. "We still don't have any proof of the macaws," Tulio said.

Linda nodded. "I don't know how we're going to figure out–"

"Going somewhere?" A group of loggers stepped out of the jungle in front of them. They were surrounded. The foreman waited for an answer to his question.

"Yeah, uhhh, we're just, umm, trying to catch our tour to go zip-lining. Whee! Have you ever tried it?"

A man in a white suit stepped forward. "Your tour is over. Welcome to ours."

Blu flew to Linda and Tulio's camp, noticing the crates that were marked for Tulio's conservatory. "Linda! Tulio!" But they were nowhere to be found. What he did find, though, were all the creature comforts of home that he'd been missing. Like food you didn't have to hunt for.

"Oh, I miss this," Blu said, looking around. He spotted a small framed photo on a side table. It was of Jewel, Blu, and the kids perched near Linda and Tulio back in Rio.

Blu felt tears forming. His shoulders sagged. He'd been a fool.

Leaves rustled nearby. "Linda?" Blu called hopefully. He pulled himself together and took off toward the village. Suddenly he was tackled out of the air. He landed hard on the ground. Roberto stood over him. He looked disgusted.

"Eduardo was right! Traitor! You are not to be trusted! Human sympathizer! Everything you have–and you do *this*."

Blu gaped at him. "What are you talking about? You're the one who's Mr. Perfect. Perfect voice, perfect dance moves, perfect wingspan."

Roberto pushed the words aside. "All meaningless. You have the real treasure–a family. What I wouldn't give to be you. Only I'm not a traitor! Throwing it all away for a *Linda*!"

"Whoa, whoa, whoa. Wait! You don't understand!" Blu said hotly.

"There are no good humans!" Roberto shouted. "They lure you in! They trap you!" Roberto lifted up some feathers on his leg, revealing a small metal band. "They did this!"

Blu looked at him, stunned.

"Next thing you know, you're in a cage, walking up and down a tiny ladder. They destroy your mind!" Roberto was out of control. "Polly want a cracker? Polly want a cracker? Polly want a cracker? No! Enough crackers! I hate crackers!"

He was still ranting when a huge logging harvester crashed through the dense underbrush, heading right at them.

"It's them! It's them!" Roberto shrieked, frozen in place in full-on panic mode.

The harvester made a horrible, deafening noise as it barreled toward the birds. Without taking time to think, Blu flew into Roberto, pushing him out of the way and saving his life.

"C'mon! Roberto!" he yelled as the harvester destroyed the camp, crushing everything in its path. He and Roberto flew out of the way and landed on a high branch.

Roberto was hyperventilating. "Not again. Not again! No more crackers!"

Blu slapped him hard. "Snap out of it!" he commanded, shocked to see Mr. Perfect turn into a blubbering mess.

Below them the harvester continued to grind away. "Look, we've got one chance to stop this, okay?" Blu said. "I have to find my friends. You fly back and warn the others. Got it?"

"Yeah, I got it," Roberto said, pulling himself together.

Blu nodded. "Okay. Go!" And the two birds flew off in opposite directions.

Eduardo and Aunt Mimi were deep in conversation. "You could talk to Felipe, work something–"

"Never. He's not a guy that wants to listen to reason," Eduardo told her.

"Felipe's not the only one," Aunt Mimi said knowingly.

Eduardo gritted his beak. "Everything had been going perfectly until that . . . that dimwit–" He stopped. Jewel was standing right in front of him.

"Daddy–"

Roberto flew up to them. "Humans! Loggers! The lights! The lights!" He gasped, spinning in circles.

Eduardo slapped him across the face. "Get ahold of yourself!"

Roberto took a steadying breath. "The loggers are coming and Blu is with them."

This was too much for Eduardo. "Traitor! I knew you couldn't trust a bird raised by humans."

"No, no, no!" Roberto corrected. "Blu is trying to help us!"

Jewel gasped. "What? By himself?"

Explosions boomed off in the distance. Jewel knew what this meant: the loggers were getting closer. The other macaws began to cry out in fear as smoke rose on the horizon.

"Okay, pack up the kids, we're leaving," Eduardo

announced firmly. "Let's go! Everyone move out! Go, go!"

Jewel hesitated, searching for the right words. "Dad! Dad . . . I'm not going with you."

"You have to go with me!" Eduardo cried. "I will not let my family be in danger again."

"Blu is our family now, too!" Jewel cried.

"I can't stand the thought of losing you again," Eduardo told her, full of emotion.

"I can't lose Blu. I love you, Dad," Jewel said.

"We're going with you." It was Tiago.

But Jewel shook her head. "No, baby, you can't. It's too dangerous. But I want you to stick together, stay with Pop-Pop! And Daddy and I will find you, okay?

Eduardo stood tall and turned to the tribe. "Okay, move out! Let's go!" More explosions sounded in the distance.

"Doomed! Over!" Roberto cried, freaking out again.

Aunt Mimi smacked him.

"Oww!" Roberto yelped. "Why does everybody keep doing that?"

Things were not looking good for Tulio and Linda. They were tied to a huge tree.

"Your left . . . your right," Linda whispered. They were working together, using the ropes and their legs to shimmy their way up the tree.

"And your right leg, my left leg . . . good!" Linda said. "Good, good, good! Now go up!" Sweat poured down their faces. Their hands intertwined around the tree.

Tulio squinted upward, into the sun, and saw vultures circling overhead. "Linda, I am so sorry. This is all my fault."

Linda swallowed. "As bad as this is . . . there's nowhere else I'd rather be than with you. Even if it is tied to a tree." His fingers gave hers a reassuring squeeze.

Squawk!

"Jewel! Jewel! Down here!" Linda cried as Jewel swooped down in front of them. "Jewel! What are you doing here? It's dangerous!"

Jewel landed between them and expertly picked the knots apart. Soon Tulio and Linda were free!

"Thank you. Let's follow her!" Linda said as Jewel started off in the direction of the logging noises. She flew faster than they could follow on foot.

"I told you I heard him," Linda told her husband, joyful.

Blu flew high above the treetops. He could hear the sound of loggers in the distance. Ahead was a clearing where all the trees had been cut down. It looked like a war zone.

Up ahead was an area of clear-cut forest just off the logging road. He realized that this wasn't far from the macaw village.

Time was running out.

This was a big-time operation. The foreman drove a big truck, talking animatedly on the radio to his crew. A bulldozer headed through the brush, pushing smaller trees down. Blu landed and looked around, feeling helpless. What could one little bird do against all this?

"Think of something," he urged himself. And when a huge harvester came straight at him, Blu did the only thing he could think of. He flew into the cab and yanked the keys from the ignition. "Hey!" The driver grabbed him.

But Jewel was there. She swooped in and smacked the driver on the side of his face. *Boink!* The driver let Blu go and Blu and Jewel flew out of reach.

Trees were falling all around them. And there, in the middle of it all, were Linda and Tulio.

Blu flew straight for Linda, landing on her shoulder. And as the bulldozer roared toward them, Linda and Tulio locked hands. Blu feared the worst–but the bulldozer finally stopped, just inches from Tulio. The driver was staring at something—and when Blu saw what it was, his heart swelled with pride: the entire flock of blue macaws, hundreds of them, ready to fight for the jungle.

"Dad!" Jewel cried.

"Birds of blue feathers," Eduardo began.

"Have to stick together!" Carla, Bia, and Tiago finished.

"Get them!" Eduardo shouted, and Blu knew they were all in this together now. The birds swarmed to attack the loggers, who hid behind their machines.

"It's on, baby!" Pedro cried as Carla led the talent-show animals into battle.

Rocks rained down on the machines, denting roofs, jamming truck tracks, and plugging exhaust pipes. The excavator roared into action, uprooting a tree and swinging it toward the birds.

Then, a bulldozer clipped Eduardo, knocking him to the ground. Blu watched as a bulldozer's shovel moved toward him. But before the shovel could strike, it was grabbed by an excavator's claw: Linda was in the driver's seat!

The two machines battled for supremacy—until Felipe arrived with the red macaws.

The red macaws pelted the machine with seed pods, giving Linda the leverage she needed to tip the bulldozer over. The birds banded together to destroy the machines, unscrewing bolts and sticking coconuts in tailpipes. Together, the two tribes created a purple, swirling squadron of angry birds.

But it wasn't over yet. A tree fell, and behind it was the big boss, holding a match to a fuse that was connected to sticks of dynamite tied to every tree.

"Hey! No pyrotechnics without parental permission!" Tiago shouted as he manned a construction claw. He scooped the boss up—but the man managed to drop a lit match, which landed on the fuse, lighting it.

As the flame made its way up the fuse, Blu made a decision: he grabbed the dynamite string with his beak and flew with it into the sky.

"Blu, no!" Jewel cried, frightened.

Once Blu was above the trees, he used his best soccer kick to knock the dynamite away from his body . . . *Boom!* A huge explosion lit up the sky. Smoke enveloped Blu as he fell . . .

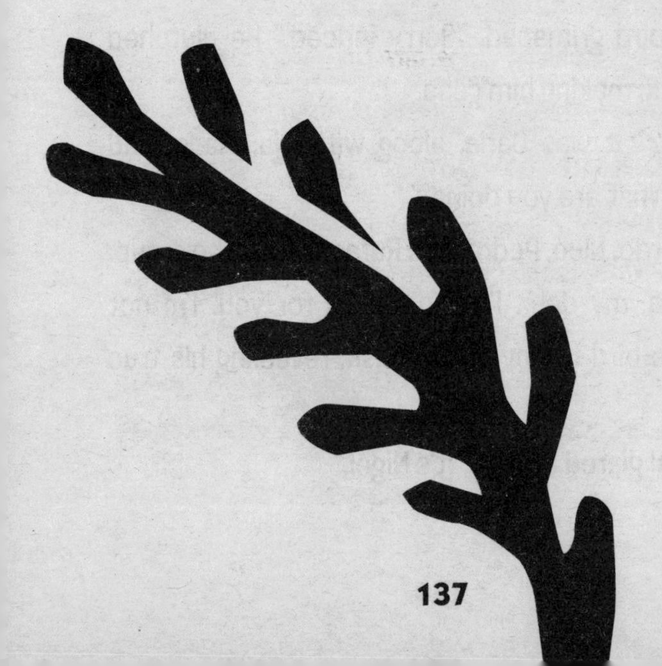

Chapter 13

"Hello. How's it dangling?"

Blu blinked. He was upside down, tangled in vines below the treetops. A bird wearing a mask was next to him. "Where's Jewel?" Blu mumbled. "The kids?"

"Not to worry, Blu," the bird told him. "I will soon relieve you of your domestic duties."

Blu blinked again. "Sorry–do I know you?"

The bird grimaced. "Sorry indeed." He clutched Blu's neck, making him gasp.

"Bob?" It was Carla, along with Bia, Tiago, and Jewel. "What are you doing?"

Eduardo, Nico, Pedro, and Rafael joined the group.

"Carla, my dear, I've got news for you. I'm not Bob." The bird removed his mask, revealing his true identity.

Jewel glared at him. "It's Nigel."

"Who the heck is Nigel?" Eduardo asked, studying the cockatoo.

Nigel grabbed Blu by the throat again and held out a threatening wing. "Wait! An audience at last!" As more birds and other animals arrived, Nigel relished the attention. "Never hath a cockatoo endured such pain at the hands of so wretched a blue macaw."

In the distance, Gabi and Charlie recognized Nigel. "It's happening," Gabi whispered.

"Alas, poor Blu, I knew him well," Nigel went on. "You will pay a painful price for your pestilence."

No one saw Charlie take aim with a quill pointed directly at Blu's heart.

"Steady," Gabi cautioned under her breath.

"My ashes, as the phoenix, have brought forth a bird that will revenge upon you all," Nigel went on, stepping forward.

Blu looked at Nigel, then Eduardo, remembering his father-in-law's words of wisdom. "My beak is my most important tool," he whispered. In one swift motion, he lifted himself up and used his beak to cut himself free. Then he charged Nigel. The two birds were in the middle of a fierce battle of wing-to-wing combat.

In the distance, Gabi was trying to capture Blu in Charlie's gun sight, but the macaw was moving around too quickly. But then Nigel pushed Blu back, giving Gabi and Charlie a clear shot.

"Shoot! Shoot!" Gabi urged. Just as Charlie shot the quill, Nigel lunged toward Blu. Then he froze, a look of painful surprise on his face. Nigel gasped and rolled over on the ground.

Gabi gasped. "Nigel!" She raced to his side.

"Hard to speak," Nigel managed to say. "Is this the end? So, so, so soon. I was too young, too talented, too beautiful to live." His voice was weak. "My final curtain call, and it's standing room only."

Gabi was dripping with poison. She watched, appalled, as Nigel let out a last dramatic breath. His eyes closed and his head flopped motionless to the side.

"Nooooo!" she wailed. "No! What have I done? What have I done? I can't live without you! If I cannot liveth with thee, then I shall not liveth at all!" She gulped. "I just came up with that." Then, she pushed a drop of poison out of her finger, drank it, and instantly fell lifeless across Nigel's chest.

The others watched in stunned silence. Someone began a slow clap, and a smattering of applause followed.

"That frog is not a poisonous dart frog," Bia said. "The poisonous ones have red spots on their backs. Everybody knows that."

One of the cockatoo's eyes opened. "What?"

Gabi opened both of her eyes. "What?"

Nigel drew in a breath. "We're not . . . dead?"

Gabi was blinking very quickly. "But, my parents always told me I was toxic and should never touch anything," she said, mystified.

"Wow, so you're not poisonous," Carla spoke up. "You just had really mean parents."

Nigel rushed toward Blu, but fell flat on his face. Gabi held tight to his legs. "Oh, wow," Gabi said, snuggling into Nigel. "So now, we can be together, my Nigel Wigel Wiggle Wumps. I'm never gonna let you go. Gimme a kiss."

"Good luck with that," Blu said. He and the others flew off, leaving the frog and the cockatoo alone.

Nigel's mind was not on romance. "Wait, wait! Come back!" he shouted as all of the animals left him and Gabi alone together. "You'll pay for this, Blu!"

Jewel leaned her head on Blu's shoulder. "So it's settled? We'll make the jungle our home. . . ."

"But spend summers and the occasional weekend back in Rio," Blu finished for her.

Jewel smiled. "Thank you, Blu. This means so much to me. You're still my one and only."

"Even if I'm not the only other one?" he asked.

Jewel laughed. "Especially because you're not!"

Blu smiled brightly. "Hmmm, I'm not sure I believe

you," he said coyly. "You should probably come closer." Jewel took a dutiful step forward.

"Closer." She took another step forward, her eyes twinkling. Blu looked at her. "I'm going to kiss you now."

And he did.

Several days later, the TV news stations continued to air full coverage of the amazing events that had taken place in the forest. "It was bird vs. machine in the Amazon jungle earlier this week as these rare macaws put the *wild* in wildlife," reported a female TV news anchor. People all over Rio were watching the coverage. The footage switched to an interview the news anchor had conducted with Linda and Tulio. "Dr. Montiero, what a journey, from Rio to the Amazon. What's next for these beautiful creatures?"

"With the discovery of these rare macaws, the entire area will be protected as a national wildlife refuge," Tulio told the reporter. A few macaws flew over and landed on the news anchor.

"Oh, hey, hi guys. Hi," she told them as they played with her hair. "Oh, hey, not the hair. I think you want to help me kick off Carnaval . . . *Como celebrar!*"

It was Carnaval time again, and the macaw village was rocking out! The talent show was a massive success. Creatures were getting down and having fun. The rhythms were sweet, the dancing was over the top, the parade floats were incredible, and the party atmosphere was contagious. And in the middle of it, Blu and his family and friends were having a blast.

Blu couldn't stop smiling as he danced the night away. He had Jewel. He had his children. His friends. His freedom. The wild.

Blu had it all!